Bear Creek

Ben Tobin had ridden for Wells Fargo for two hard years. He'd chased after no-goods riding the owl-hoot trail, survived shootouts, and slept beneath the stars more times than he cared to remember. But then his partner was badly wounded and Tobin decided to call time on his riding days. However, when his old partner looks him up to ask him for his help, it's a request he can't ignore.

Now, he finds himself riding into trouble once again. Short-trigger men stalk the alleyways of Bear Creek. Powerful ranchers are playing a dangerous game, calculating there is big money for the taking. Hired killers target Tobin and he'll need all his old skills with his Navy Colt to survive. . . .

Bear Creek

Jack Edwardes

A Black Horse Western

ROBERT HALE · LONDON

ISBN 978-0-7090-9069-4

Robert Hale Limited
Clerkenwell House
Clerkenwell Green
London EC1R 0HT

www.halebooks.com

Typeset by
Derek Doyle & Associates, Shaw Heath
Printed and bound in Great Britain by
CPI Antony Rowe, Chippenham and Eastbourne

CHAPTER ONE

Ben Tobin heard the scream as he was kicking out the ashes of the fire which had heated his coffee, a chunk of good meat and a couple of eggs. He tensed for a moment, his hand dropping to the butt of his Navy Colt, then he relaxed. Some creature just like himself taking its breakfast, he decided. He checked the embers of his fire were dead before threading his way through the cotton trees which had sheltered him for the night. As Tobin approached his palomino, saddled at first light, the animal raised its head from the thin grass that grew beneath the shade of the branches.

He unhitched the palomino's reins from one of the trees and swung easily into the saddle, ducking to avoid the low hanging branches. He allowed the animal its head as it threaded a way between the trees. Twenty yards further and he broke out of the ring of trees, upright in his saddle, breathing in deeply the sharp morning air. Then he heard the scream once more.

'That's a woman,' he said aloud.

His Plains spurs gently touched the palomino's sides. Fifty yards at a trot took him to the edge of the high ground where he could look down on the trail to Bear Creek. An empty buggy stood on the dirt of the trail. Beyond, in an open meadow, a woman was being pushed between two men. As she fought to keep her balance she was being turned by one man and pushed back to the other, only for him to send her staggering back. The raucous laughter from the two men cut through the air.

Tobin drew his Winchester from its scabbard. He'd find out later what all this was about; right now he'd call a halt. He levered his long gun ready to fire before taking aim. His finger squeezed the trigger; dirt and buffalo grass spurted a few feet from the man who spun around to lift his face in Tobin's direction.

Tobin urged his mount forward down the slope and across the trail into the meadow, pushing his long gun into its scabbard and drawing his Navy Colt as he crossed over the trail. The woman had slumped to the ground, sobbing loudly, her head down and her long dark hair brushing the cotton of her blue skirt.

'Don't try anythin'!' Tobin shouted.

The shorter of the two men moved his hand quickly away from the butt of his sidearm as a slug from Tobin's Colt smacked into the ground five feet from his boot. Tobin reined in his mount, the palomino skittering across the buffalo grass.

'What the hell's goin' on here?'

'We wuz just havin' some fun. We weren't gonna hurt the lady.'

The speaker, whose face bore a knife scar, slurred his words, and after a moment Tobin slid his Colt into its holster. Both men were liquored up cowboys, he realized. He'd make them apologise to the woman and send them packing. He turned to the other.

'How 'bout you? You just havin' fun?'

'That's right, mister.'

6

The cowboy nodded several times as if his jerking head would convince Tobin he was on the level. The sour smell of liquor came from his open mouth. Tobin turned away and walked slowly across to where the woman sat on the ground.

'You're safe now, ma'am,' he said softly.

He leaned forward to help her stand and as he did so he registered a movement from the corner of his eye. He pivoted on the heel of his boot, drawing his Colt in one easy movement. His sidearm kicked back into the palm of his hand. The scarred cowboy stared down, his mouth agape as blood spurted from his arm. He shouted a curse as he fell backwards on to the ground, his sidearm falling to the ground.

Tobin spun around. 'You gonna try anythin'?'

The cowboy, staring with bulging eyes at the Colt in Tobin's fist, shook his head. Colour had drained from his weather-beaten features.

'I ain't gonna be any trouble, mister,' he said.

'Then get this damn fool on to his horse and hightail outta here afore I change my mind 'bout plugging both of you.'

'Sure, mister, sure.'

His eyes never left Tobin as he scuttled towards his companion and heaved him to his feet. Tobin held his Colt down by his side as he watched the two men reach their horses and mount up. Behind him the woman had become quiet. The cowboys didn't look back as they kicked their horses forward. Tobin watched them gallop across the meadow, satisfied they would not return.

He turned back to the woman to find her standing a few feet away, scrubbing at her face with a square of white linen. Her cheeks were pale and her brow furrowed. As she became aware of his steady gaze she dropped her head but not before he caught the shadow of what could have happened pass across her eyes.

'They'll not be back,' he said, keeping his voice soft.

She raised her head. 'I have to thank you, sir, for your help.'

'The name's Tobin, ma'am. I'm glad I came along.'

'I'm not sure what they. . . .'

'Don't dwell on it, ma'am,' Tobin cut in. He put out an arm to steady the woman as she took a pace forward and staggered slightly. 'Here, take my arm an' we'll get you back to your buggy.'

Slowly, the woman's hand resting lightly on Tobin's arm, they walked the thirty yards across the meadow back to the trail, the palomino's reins held loosely in Tobin's free hand. Ten yards from the buggy Tobin broke the silence.

'You live in Bear Creek, ma'am?'

'Yes, I do.' She turned her face to look up at him. Colour had come back to her face, and her brow had cleared of the worried frown. 'Excuse my poor manners, Mr Tobin. My name is Elizabeth Summers.' She paused for a moment. 'And you, Mr Tobin,' she said. 'What brings you to Bear Creek?'

He shrugged his shoulders. 'Guess I'm just driftin' for a time. I've no kinfolk, nothin' to hold me in any place.'

They had reached the buggy standing on the trail and Tobin grabbed the chance to avoid saying more. 'Mebbe it's better I ride in the buggy with you. That's if you've no objection, ma'am,' he added quickly. 'Just seems sensible I drive the pony until you're feelin' yourself agin.'

'I'd like that, Mr Tobin. I confess I still feel out of sorts.'

He handed her into the seat before securing the palomino at the rear of the buggy, and then taking his seat alongside the woman. He tapped the pony's back with the reins and the animal moved forward causing the buggy to shudder for a moment as its wheels were released from the loose earth of the trail.

'How long to Bear Creek, ma'am?'

'Maybe half an hour.' She pointed out the trunk of a tree that lay a few yards from the trail. 'I can judge the time from this spot.'

Tobin held the reins loosely, content to let the pony decide on its own pace. 'You make this trip often?'

'Twice a week to the Ruskin homestead. I was late last night and Mrs Ruskin kindly offered hospitality.'

Her voice was even and Tobin guessed she was already recovering from her experience. Tougher than she looked, he decided. And though she was past the first bloom of youth she was still an attractive woman.

'Their daughter Emma has a talent for music,' she continued. 'Mr Ruskin raised the money to buy her a pianoforte.' Aware that Tobin had turned his head to look at her, she added, 'Mr Ruskin can't afford to send Emma to Cheyenne for lessons so when I came to Bear Creek two years ago I agreed to help.'

Tobin was about to ask more questions but before he could speak Elizabeth cut in. 'That wasn't just luck back there in the meadow,' she said.

Tobin frowned. 'I'm not sure I'm followin' you, ma'am.'

'You could have killed that cowboy when he pulled his gun on you. Nobody in Wyoming would have blamed you. But you didn't.'

Tobin shrugged. 'He was drunk an' stupid. No sense in killin' a man for that.'

She gave a brief nod. Then, as they both turned to look ahead along the trail, the sound of galloping horses came from around the bend maybe three hundred yards ahead. The buggy had moved another fifty yards when a group of around fifteen riders came into view. They were led by a rider dressed all in black save for his stylish Stetson. A sheriff's star pinned to his black leather vest glinted in the early morning sun. As the group of riders pounded towards the buggy, Tobin saw the sheriff draw his sidearm and, with a stiff extended arm, aim in the buggy's direction. Tobin hauled on the pony's reins bringing the buggy to a shuddering halt.

Elizabeth clutched at Tobin's arm. 'What's happening?' she said. 'That's Sheriff Devlin.'

'Tobin! I wanna see your hands all the time,' shouted Devlin as he spurred his mount forward alongside the buggy. The warm air from the mouth of Devlin's horse hit Tobin in the face as Devlin leaned forward in the saddle and loomed over him.

'You're gonna spend time in jail, Tobin. A long, long time.'

He leaned back in his saddle seemingly content that Tobin hadn't moved. 'Don't you be scared, Miss Summers,' he said, his sidearm now held loosely alongside his leg. 'But I sure don't know what you're about with this no-good. He fancy-talked you into somethin', I bet.'

'Mr Tobin helped me in a desperate situation, Mr Devlin. Are you sure there's no mistake?'

Instead of replying immediately, Devlin shoved his hand beneath his vest and pulled out a roll of rough paper. He shook it open, holding it so Elizabeth could see it clearly. Above the bold black letters proclaiming 'Ben Tobin Wanted for Murder' Tobin's features were instantly recognizable from the artist's impression.

Devlin shoved the poster back beneath his vest. 'Unbuckle the gunbelt, Tobin, and step down from the buggy.' Without turning he called to one of the men behind him. 'Charlie, get Tobin on his horse. If he tries to escape, shoot him. An'

10

don't give him any chances. Tobin can shoot the eye out of a hawk at fifty paces.'

Wordlessly, Elizabeth touched Tobin's arm. Tobin didn't look at her as he gave her the pony's reins before unbuckling his gunbelt, then handing it across to Devlin.

The sheriff backed his mount a few feet, allowing Tobin to step down to the trail and move to the rear of the buggy to unhitch his palomino. Tobin mounted his horse, conscious of Elizabeth's gaze as she turned to look at him. With a grim smile on his weather-beaten features he raised a finger to the brim of his hat in a salute and moved his palomino between the two riders who would escort him to Bear Creek.

Tobin pushed himself up from his bunk as he heard someone open the door from Devlin's office. The uneven steps of the old-timer who worked around the jail sounded along the short passageway which led to the two cages. Supper time, and Tobin guessed that nothing was about to change. For three nights Tobin had eaten bread and beans and his stomach ached for a good steak. He stood up as the old-timer reached his door. Then he had a pleasant surprise.

'Hey, Skippy! What you got there?'

The old man grunted. 'Reckon you fooled one honest citizen. Miss Summers sent this in for you, an' Mr Devlin says it's okay to give it you.'

Across the passage the other prisoner lifted his head from his bunk and sniffed the air. His dirty pants and shirt and the smell of sweat that arose from him showed he'd been a prisoner for some while. He moved quickly to the front of his cage, showing blackened teeth in a greedy leer.

'Tobin! You gonna gimme a piece o' that pie?'

'You heard what Skippy said, the pie's for me.'

'Nobody's gettin' nuthin' if you two scallywags don't get

11

back to your bunks. I ain't openin' the doors afore you do,' Skippy growled. 'Now go on back, both o' you.'

Tobin backed away from the bars and lowered himself to the bunk again, his eyes never leaving the pie on the metal tray. Both men watched Skippy as he placed the tray on the floor and unlocked the door to Tobin's cage.

'Hey! You really want some o' this pie?' Tobin called across the passageway.

'I sure do! That'd be mighty kind o' you.'

'You wanna lend a knife, Skippy,' Tobin asked. 'So I can cut the pie?'

'You take me fer a damn fool?' Skippy said, stepping through the doorway. 'You wanna cut the pie, use the fork.'

He set the plate of beans and the pie at the end of Tobin's bunk, placing the tin mug of hot black coffee in Tobin's out-stretched hand. With his free hand Tobin groped around beneath the straw-filled pillow behind him and took out his fork. He held the tines in his hand and used the handle to cut out a large slice in the soft pastry.

He held up the slice of pie to Skippy. 'Pie comin' over,' he called to the other prisoner.'

'I sure do thank you, Tobin!'

A few minutes later Skippy had given both prisoners their suppers and left them alone. Tobin found even the beans tasted better with the anticipation of the pie. No sense in keeping it, he decided, breaking the pie in half, sipping his coffee and munching away until the pie was finished.

He reached in the top of his shirt and pulled out a small muslin bag of tobacco hung around his neck on a thin cord. From the pocket of his vest he took a paper and the one match Devlin allowed him each day. A minute later he was breathing in the rough tobacco.

'That was mighty fine pie,' the other prisoner called. 'You

gonna talk with me now? You ain't said a word these last three days.'

Tobin drew on his roll-up, leaning back against the stucco wall. 'Guess I'll mebbe talk some,' he said. 'Pass the time.' He looked across to where the other prisoner had moved close to the bars of his cage. 'Whaddya say your name was?'

'Bart Masefield.'

Tobin came off his bunk to stand against the bars of his own cage, staring across the passageway. 'I'll be damned! You any kin to Frank Masefield?'

'He's my brother! You know Frank?'

Tobin shook his head. 'I just took a week tryin' to track him down. Feller I know down in Colorado said he was a good man to work for.' He paused, his face grim. 'Mebbe I got told wrong. You bein' his brother an' all, an' in this place.'

'You ain't been told wrong, Tobin. Frank knows his business. We hit the bank down in Morgantown. Got the money an' nobody stopped lead. Then a goddamned sod-buster shot down my horse as we were gettin' away. I never stood no chance. Damn townfolk woulda torn me to pieces if the sheriff hadna been around.'

Tobin frowned. 'Morgan's some way. I rode through there a coupla days back. How come you're here?'

'They reckoned the jail wouldna held me. Frank woulda bust me out.' Masefield spat into the bucket by his bunk. 'No chance o' that 'round these parts with that sonovabitch Devlin.'

'You know where your brother's holed up?'

'Sure I do but I ain't sayin' nothin'.'

Tobin almost smiled. He lowered his voice so that Masefield had to strain forward to hear what was said. 'I gotta deal for you, Bart. I get us both outta here an' you an' me join up with your brother.'

'An' how the hell you gonna do that?'

Tobin's voice dropped even lower to a hoarse whisper. 'Pin your ears back, Bart. This is the way we're gonna fix it.'

'Sheriff! Sheriff Devlin!'

Masefield's shout echoed along the passageway as he stood at the bars of his cage looking across to where Tobin lay on his bunk, holding his stomach and groaning loudly.

'Sheriff!' Masefield shouted again. 'You gotta take a look at Tobin. He's sick, I tellya!'

The door from Devlin's office was flung open and the sheriff stood framed in the doorway. He held up an oil lamp, throwing yellow light along the night-time gloom of the passage.

'You stop that yellin', Masefield,' he rasped. 'I hear you agin an' you ain't gonna get chow tomorrow.'

'Tobin's sick, Sheriff,' Masefield protested. 'Mebbe there was somethin' wrong with that pie.'

'What the hell you sayin'?'

Devlin advanced down the passageway and peered into Tobin's cage. Loud groans and choking noises came from Tobin. His bootless feet drummed on the end of his bunk. Devlin muttered a curse.

'Guess he's in bad shape,' he admitted. 'But I ain't gettin' the doc outta his bed for a no-good like Tobin.' He placed the lamp on the rough wooden table which stood to the side of the cages and from his belt he took the key to Tobin's cage. He took his sidearm from its holster and held it by his side while he unlocked the door. As he stepped inside the cage Tobin let out a long groan, froth bubbling around his lips in his contorted face.

'What the hell's wrong, Tobin?'

14

Devlin approached the bunk and leaned over Tobin, peering through the shadows thrown by the lamp outside the cage.

'You gotta—' Devlin's voice was cut off abruptly as Tobin's hand shot from beneath the rough blanket and grasped him by the throat. With a grunt Tobin heaved Devlin down on top of him, shoving a .22 pistol hard into his belly.

'Drop the iron, Devlin! Or you're gonna die real hard!'

Tobin's face was barely six inches away from Devlin's, and he could detect the sweetish smell of the whiskey the sheriff had drunk before taking over from his deputy.

'I ain't gonna say it agin! Drop the iron!'

There was a thump on the floor beside the bunk. Devlin attempted a strangled curse. 'You're gonna hang for this, Tobin!'

Slowly, Tobin released his grasp from Devlin's throat. 'Now back away. I ain't of a mind to shoot you but you try anythin' an' I will.'

'Shoot the bastard, Tobin! Shoot him!'

Tobin didn't take his eyes off Devlin as the sheriff pushed himself off the bunk and backed away to the wall of the cage. 'Shut your goddamned mouth, Masefield!' Tobin rasped. 'Or you're gonna stay where you are.'

Holding the small pistol in his hand, Tobin bent and picked up the Colt Devlin had dropped. He pushed the small pistol into the belt of his pants and spat out the sliver of rough soap he'd saved that morning, before wiping the sleeve of his shirt across his mouth.

'Toss across the keys,' he ordered Devlin. 'Be smart! We get outta this place, you'll see the sun come up tomorrow.'

He watched as Devlin eased the jail keys from his belt and tossed them across. Without looking down, Tobin reached for his boots which stood beside his bunk. Aiming the Colt at

Devlin, and carrying his boots, he moved to the door of the cage.

'You gonna leave him to holler?' Masefield said hoarsely.

Tobin stepped into the passageway and turned to lock the door. 'He ain't gonna wake folks at this time,' he said, as he bent to pull on his boots. 'No sense in harmin' a lawman when you don't have to.'

'Then open up an' let me outta here!'

Tobin stood up to stare hard at Masefield. 'We still got that deal?'

'I tol' you! Now let me outta here!'

After checking the sheriff's office was empty the two men rushed to grab their gunbelts from the deep drawer in Devlin's desk. Tobin threw the pocket pistol on to the desk, and strode to the door. The town was still; only a couple of lights showed from clapboards at the end of Main Street.

'Jesus! Must be our lucky night!' Mansfield said gleefully. 'There's a place I know we can hole up afore daybreak.'

He pointed at the two horses hitched to the rail on the other side of the street. Both men jumped the steps down to the hardpack of the street and ran to the horses. Moments later they were riding at full gallop out of town.

CHAPTER TWO

Tobin opened his eyes, aware of the flickering shadows around the fire he and Masefield had set several hours before. He didn't have to guess what had woken him – the steel barrel of a handgun was pressed against the side of his head. He attempted to turn his head but the gun was pushed harder, causing the gunsight to nick his skin.

'Make a move an' I kill you now.'

'Hey, Bart! What the hell you doin'?'

'Shut your goddamned mouth,' rasped Masefield. 'I'm gonna back off an' you get to your feet. You go for your belt under that blanket an' I'm gonna shoot you down right now.'

'Take it easy Bart. You got this all wrong. You an' me we're partners. I wanna work for your brother that's all.'

'I tol' you. I ain't gonna tell you agin. Shut your mouth an' get on your feet.'

'OK, Bart. Take it easy.'

Tobin shrugged off the blanket which had kept him warm during the cool night. Any move for his gunbelt would prompt Masefield to shoot. As he scrambled to his feet he knew he was going to have to do some fast talking. In the flickering shadows he saw Masefield put a hand to his face.

'You know what this is, Tobin?' Masefield said.

'Your nose, I reckon.'

'You're goddamned right. My nose. I ain't lettered like Frank but I got my nose. An' it never lets me down. An' it tells me I ain't got a handle on you an' me gettin' outta jail.'

'Bart, all you gotta do is ask. Put the gun away an' we'll talk it over.'

'You ain't sweet-talkin' me. Why you so damned struck on gettin' to Ellisville? You a bounty hunter after Frank?'

Tobin breathed in. He had the information he needed. Now all he had to do was to stay alive. 'No, I ain't a bounty hunter. I'm just—'

'Where'd you get that little popgun you held on Devlin?' Masefield cut in.

'It was in my boot.'

'You're lyin', Tobin! Sheriff had me stripped down afore I got put in that cage. He does it to all his prisoners.'

Masefield tensed; the sound of the breeze rustling the leaves of the cottonwoods was cut by the metallic click of Masefield cocking his sidearm. Tobin felt the bile rise to the back of his throat.

'Take it easy, Bart! You an' me. We're partners, ain't we?'

A shot rang out and for a moment both men were still, their torsos rigid as if held by giant fists. Then Masefield took a pace forward, his arm dropped to his side, and he pitched forward, face first, on to the buffalo grass.

Tobin sucked in air, feeling as if his lungs were about to burst, his heart beating as if it would tear from his chest. He swallowed furiously, feeling the beans he'd eaten the previous night stirring at the bottom of his gullet. A figure dressed in black save for his cream coloured Stetson emerged from the trees, a Peacemaker held loosely by his side.

'Jesus, Josh! You left that goddamned late!'

Sheriff Devlin shoved his Peacemaker back into his holster, and walked across the clearing to the fallen

Masefield. He knelt beside the body for a few seconds before getting to his feet.

'I was hopin' he might tell us how many men Frank Masefield has with him.' He came closer to Tobin. 'You OK?'

'Yeah, I'm OK. Sonovabitch shoulda stayed grateful. He'd still be alive.'

'I'll take him back,' Devlin said. 'The town'll have to bury him. Marshal down in Cheyenne gets a mite ornery 'bout escaped prisoners. Likes to know I settled the score.'

Devlin looked around. 'You wanna give me a hand an' put this no-good on his horse?' He looked back at Tobin. 'We could put him in the ground for a few days. You know I'll ride with you to Ellisville.'

'Sure you will. You get seen, an' we'll both be in Boot Hill. Just tell me how to get there an' I'll do the rest.'

Devlin twisted his mouth. 'You'll find Masefield easy enough. Likes to dress fancy.' In the light thrown by the fire Tobin saw him smile. 'Ain't as fancy as me, though. C'mon, let's fix old Bart on my horse. You can take Bart's mount for a pack horse. Then we'll get some sleep.'

Tobin brought the buckskin to the crest of a high ridge, reining in his mount to a walk. Behind him the pack horse also slowed to a walk. Maybe half a mile away, water glistened in the noontime sun. Beyond the water, meadows were cut by a trail that led to a scattering of rough cabins. The outlines of a settlement maybe five hundred yards on from the cabins showed against the darkness of a forest. A sawmill poked up at the edge of the single storey buildings.

Tobin urged his mount forward, leaning back in his saddle as the buckskin began to pick its way down the side of the hill. The animal was a poor ride, and he regretted that his palomino was in the livery stable back in Bear Creek. He splashed through the shallow stream, both horses stepping lively, seeming to anticipate what lay ahead after a long ride. After a moment's thought Tobin dropped his hand and eased the butt of his Navy Colt. From what Josh had told him of Masefield it was as well to be on his guard as he passed the cabins.

He sped along the track, acknowledging with a wave the shout from a figure outlined in a doorway. A few minutes later he was on the hardpack of the settlement and he reined in his mount sharply, sending both animals skittering across the street in front of a large double-fronted building. A sign hanging from chains announced the Silver Lode saloon. As he turned the head of the buckskin towards the saloon three men stood up from their seats on the boardwalk.

'You always arrive in style, stranger?'

The tallest of the men had called out. He was wearing trail clothes, but his pants were unmarked and his boots gleamed with polish. Beneath his leather waistcoat the soft material of his shirt was topped with a green neckerchief which might have been silk. He was clean shaven and his teeth looked in good condition. At his hip was a Navy Colt similar to Tobin's. Unless the timbertown was full of fancy dressers this was the man he was looking for.

'You Mr Masefield?' Tobin asked as he stepped down from the saddle. 'I been chasin' after you these last weeks.'

'So why you been looking for me?'

'I'm lookin' for work,' Tobin said. 'An' we're in the same line o' business.'

'Is that right? An' what business is that?'

Tobin shrugged. 'Robbin' banks. Hittin' a stage if we know what it's carryin'.'

'An' where'd you hear that?'

'Charlie Darnett down in Truckee.'

20

Masefield raised his eyebrows. 'Hell, is he still alive?'

'Not any more, he ain't. Pinkertons caught up with him.'

Masefield nodded. 'What do folks know you by?'

'Tobin. Ben Tobin.'

'Come on up here, Tobin, and take a drink.' He turned to one of the men. 'Joe, get Janey an' we'll have some whiskey out here. Tell her I'll take some of that French wine.' He glanced down at the Navy Colt on Tobin's hip as Tobin settled into a chair. 'You any good with that?'

'I can shoot straight.'

'Is that right?' Masefield said slowly. 'You show me an' I might just find work for you.' He half turned in his chair and looked across the street. He pointed towards a post at the edge of the boardwalk. Pinned to the post was a small sign with a roughly painted white arrow showing the direction of the bathhouse.

'You see that sign? See if you can hit it from here.'

'The sheriff gonna go along with that?'

'He ain't gonna be any trouble.'

Tobin looked across the street. 'That sign ain't very big.'

'Haw. Haw. Haw!' The man who sat to the right of Frank Masefield brayed with mocking laughter. 'You wanna ride with us, Tobin, you gotta show us you can use that iron an' not your mouth.'

'Hey, Hal,' Masefield said. 'Give Tobin his chance.'

Tobin looked at the man called Hal for a moment then stood up to face across the street. 'Anyone wanna bet a buck agin me?'

'Sure.' Hal reached in the pocket of his leather vest and pulled out a coin.

'Hold this,' Tobin took a matching coin out of his pocket, turning to flip it across to the man called Joe who'd come back to his seat. Then he reached in his vest and pulled out

21

a gold coin. 'Five bucks says I can hit the letter "B" on that sign.'

Silence descended on the men as they exchanged glances. 'You ain't sayin' much, Hal,' snickered Joe. 'You ain't gotta mouth no more?'

'Five dollars it is,' Hal snarled.

Scarcely were the words spoken than Tobin drew his Navy Colt and with a moment's glance across the street fired twice. He continued to stand for a moment while he took two slugs from his belt and reloaded the Colt.

'Sure hope the sheriff ain't gonna be upset,' he said.

'I tol' you. Let me worry about the sheriff,' Masefield said slowly, staring across the street. 'Go look at that sign, Hal, an' make sure you tell me right.'

Hal stood up from his seat and went down the steps. The men watched him as he paused briefly in front of the sign before turning and coming back to where the men were sitting.

'Can Tobin shoot or is he all mouth?' Masefield asked. 'You gonna answer me?' he said sharply, as Hal remained silent.

'One in the top of the letter, one in the bottom,' Hal answered finally, and threw himself into the seat he'd vacated a few minutes before. A roar of appreciation went up from the other two. Joe thrust out a hand.

'Guess I'm holdin' the pot for Tobin here. Gimme five dollars.'

'Forget it, Hal,' Tobin said. 'I ain't takin' money from a feller I'm gonna be workin' with.'

Masefield frowned. 'I ain't said you're in yet.'

Tobin shrugged and turned to look at the saloon entrance. 'We gonna have that drink?'

'Sure we are,' said Joe quickly, as the batwing doors were

pushed open. 'Here's Janey with the makin's.'

A young woman in a tan-coloured shirt over a skirt that fell to her button-shoes, stepped on to the boardwalk. She was carrying a tray on which stood a couple of bottles and several glasses. She crossed the few feet to where the men were seated. Hal leaned forward to take the whiskey and Joe handed the shot glasses around, leaving the large glass for Masefield. The young woman glanced at Tobin before dropping her eyes and standing quietly beside Masefield who poured red wine into his glass from the second bottle.

Silently, the men raised their glasses after Hal had poured their drinks. Tobin drank his whiskey in one gulp and held out his shot glass for a refill. 'OK, I got the whiskey. I bin on the trail a long time; where do I get a woman?'

'Slow down, Tobin,' Frank said. 'First you get one thing straight. I give the orders round these parts. You obey 'em. You got that?'

'Fine with me.'

'You got any paper on you in the Territory?'

'First time I've seen Wyoming.'

'OK, you're in. Now go choose a woman.'

Tobin pointed a finger at the young woman. 'She's just fine.'

The young woman's eyes widened. 'No! I—'

'Shut your mouth, Janey,' Masefield cut in. 'Somethin' you oughtta know, Tobin. She's with me.'

Tobin looked at Masefield for a moment, drank his second whiskey, and then put his glass on the boardwalk beside his chair. He stood up and put a finger to his hat.

'Guess I'll see you fellers around some other time.'

'What the hell you doin'?' Masefield said sharply.

Tobin looked at Masefield. 'I ain't gonna work for no one who puts a woman above his men. Thataways, a feller ends up

23

gettin' hisself killed. No hard feelin's. I ain't aimin' to fight you for her. I'll just ride on outta here.'

There was silence on the boardwalk for a moment. Hal and Joe exchanged glances; Joe, taking a sip of his whiskey, looked as if he was wishing he was some place else. Janey clutched Masefield's shoulder more tightly, whispering a few words. He ignored her, staring hard at Tobin for several seconds. Then with a sharp slap he knocked Janey's hand away.

'She's yourn,' he said.

Janey gave a little scream, choking it off with a hand to her mouth. 'No! No!'

'I tol' you once! Shut your goddamned mouth!' Masefield barked. He didn't take his eyes off Tobin as Janey dropped the tray to the boardwalk and ran back through the doors of the saloon.

Tobin looked across at the sign he'd shot up, and rubbed his hand across his unshaven jaw. 'Guess I'll get cleaned up afore I come back an' party,' he said.

He stepped down to the street and walked away without looking back.

CHAPTER THREE

Tobin walked down the street towards the lights from the saloon spilling on to the boardwalk. He'd cleaned up in the bathhouse and put on the clean shirt that Devlin had left in the saddlebag of the horse he'd taken from Bear Creek. A bunk in one of the boarding houses had cost him fifty cents and he'd snatched a couple of hours' sleep: a long night stretched ahead of him and he'd need to be at his strongest. After he'd roused himself and splashed water over his face he'd walked along to the barber to rid himself of his four days' growth of stubble, then he ate a meal at the chophouse at the end of the street. When he walked back into the saloon folks would see that he was ready to have himself a really good time.

The heat generated from inside the saloon hit him in the face as he stepped up to the boardwalk and pushed through the doors. For a small settlement the saloon was bigger than he'd expected. Then he remembered the timber business – the men working the forests would visit this place on payday to let off steam. If the weather got really bad the settlement might see the cowboys who drove their cattle to Montana.

Women moved to and fro carrying drinks to the men sitting at tables with their cards. Over to his right beyond the group of men losing their money at faro he could see a couple of women sitting alone at a table. One was very young, too young to be in a saloon, he reckoned. She sat alongside an older woman who Tobin guessed was hired to keep an eye on the rest of the calico queens. He stood for a moment looking around at the saloon. There was no sign of Janey.

Tobin got a drink from one of the three Mexicans working the bar and crossed the saloon to where the two women were seated, their minds apparently only half on the cards before them. The older one, who was in danger of breaking out of the low cut red dress that barely covered her breasts, looked up as Tobin halted in front of the table.

'Where's Janey?' Tobin asked. 'Me an' her gotta party tonight.'

'You gotta be Tobin. Frank changed his mind. Says you can have any o' the gals you want.' She paused. 'Frank had to go outta town. He says you can have two if you've a mind to really have some fun.'

'Both together?'

'Sure, if that's what you want.'

Tobin took a sip of his whiskey. He looked at the young girl, then for a few moments turned his attention towards the women carrying drinks. He turned back to the table.

'What's your names?'

'This here young'un is Ruby. You can call me Belle.'

'OK, Belle. One at a time is fine. So I guess you an' me are gonna have a party.'

Belle's painted eyebrows rose almost to her hairline. Then a broad smile spread across her plump face. She pushed herself to her feet. 'You just tell Nancy I'm gonna be a while,' she ordered Ruby. 'I ain't been so lucky since that fellow from Houston rode through these parts.' She held out her arm to Tobin. 'Let's go, cowboy. I'm gonna show you a trick or two you ain't never seen in your life.'

Tobin took Belle's arm and they weaved their way between

the tables that stood grouped on the sawdust-covered floor. At the foot of the stairs Belle looked across to a broad-shouldered man who sat in one corner of the saloon, a scattergun across his knees. With a wave of her hand she gestured to the floor upstairs; and he raised a hand in acknowledgement, a broad grin across his face.

'Here we are,' Belle said, as she and Tobin reached the first room of the corridor. Tobin closed the door making sure there was nobody else in the passageway. Belle lit the lamp on the credenza before crossing to the large bed which occupied most of the room. Her hands started to fiddle with the buttons of her dress.

'You wanna give me the money first?'

Tobin crossed the room and placing his hand on her shoulder pushed her backwards on to the bed. 'Don't you bother with all that. Just tell me where I find Janey.'

He saw her blink twice and his hand shot out to cover her mouth with his hand before she could scream. He put his free hand around the back of her neck and pulled her towards him until their faces were only a few inches apart.

'You listen hard,' he said. 'You tell me where Janey is, an' you don't get hurt.' He released the back of her neck to slide out his knife from the top of his boot. 'You hold out on me, and I'm gonna cut you. You un'erstand?'

For a second or two her eyes were wide open with shock, then Tobin felt, rather than saw, her shoulders relax. It wasn't the first time, he guessed, that a man had held a knife to her.

'I'm gonna take my hand away,' he said. 'You scream an' you ain't gonna be pretty no more.'

Slowly he took his hand away from her mouth, and slid his knife back into his boot. Belle shuffled around until she was in a sitting position at the edge of the bed. She looked up at him, rubbing at her jaw where his strong fingers had held her.

'Frank Masefield will kill you for this.'

'Let me worry about that. All I want is Janey.'

'I tell you where she is, an' Frank will beat the skin off my back.'

'Then you gotta problem, Belle. You don't tell me an' I'm gonna do somethin' real bad.'

Belle hesitated, her head lowered. Then she looked up, seeing Tobin's hand drop to his boot again, his fingers closing around the handle of his knife.

'Then you gotta help me,' she said. 'Make it look as if I never had no chance to stop you.'

Tobin stood up, looking around the room. He crossed over to the high window and with one sweep of his knife cut the curtain cord as high as his arm would stretch. Then he returned to the bedside.

'I'm gonna tie you up an' make sure you ain't gonna be yellin'.' He stared hard at her. 'OK, where is she?'

'She's in the Hole.' Seeing him frown, she raised a hand. 'At the end of the corridor there's a room. Just a bunk an' a bucket. Any o' the gals give Frank trouble, that's where they go.'

'You got the keys?'

Belle scrabbled beneath the pillow behind her, and pulled out a single brass key. 'A gal can scream as loud as she likes an' she ain't gonna be heard. That's why we call it the Hole. But I'm tellin' you, mister. I ain't sure o' what you're plannin' but you leave your mark on that gal an' Frank Masefield's gonna come after you.'

Tobin didn't reply. Instead he pushed Belle back on the bed and roughly turned her over. A few moments later she was hogtied, the curtain rope secured around her ankles and her hands, and lashed to the heavy wood of the bed. Tobin raised his hand and undid his neckerchief.

'Here,' he said. 'You can show Masefield you ain't lyin' when you tell him what I did.'

He kneeled on the edge of the bed and looped the neck-erchief over Belle's head, thrusting one corner into her mouth before knotting two ends tightly at the back of her neck. 'Keep breathin' through your nose,' he said. 'You ain't gonna hurt.'

Tobin stood up from the bed, glancing down to reassure himself that the woman was unable to free herself. For a few seconds he listened to her breathing through her nose. Then he reached in a pocket of his vest and pulled out a couple of gold coins.

'Hate to think you're gonna hold all this agin me,' he said, thrusting the coins down the front of her dress, feeling against the back of his hand the moisture of the sweat on her breasts. A moment later he was closing the door to Belle's room behind him.

The noise and smells of the men and women below reached him as he stepped quietly along the deserted passageway. He reached the door of the room at the end, glancing behind to check that no one was coming up the stairs from the saloon. The key he'd got from Belle slid smoothly into the well oiled lock. Then he quickly stepped into the dimly lit room, and locked the door behind him. In the corner of the room Janey sat with crossed legs on the bunk. As Tobin advanced into the room she pressed herself back against the wall.

'Don't you touch me!'

Her eyeballs bulged with fear, and Tobin could see her hands shaking, her long pale fingers tugging at a thin shift, the only clothing she was wearing. Moving slowly and delib-erately, Tobin advanced into the room.

'Don't be afraid, Janey.' Tobin said softly. 'I've been sent

29

by Sheriff Devlin to take you home.'

There was a moment's silence while she took in his words. Then a flicker of defiance showed in her eyes. 'You're lyin'! It's a trick to make me like you. I saw you. You were drinkin' with Frank an' those other men.'

This was proving tougher than Tobin had expected: Masefield or his men could come into the saloon at any moment. Maybe Frank or one of the others would come up to check on Janey or wonder why Belle was absent from the saloon. He thrust his hand into his pocket, and held up the locket Devlin had given him.

'You know what this is?'

Janey scuffled across the top of the bed to reach out a hand. 'That belongs to my ma!'

He pushed it towards her and Janey snatched it from him, holding the gold-coloured locket against her breasts.

'OK, you believe me now?'

'But Frank—'

'Frank was gonna give you to a stranger. He don't give a damn for you.' Tobin didn't give her a chance to think or say any more. He stepped to the bed and grasped her by the arm. 'I got two horses outside, an' a slicker you can put over that shift. You got a back way outta here?'

Janey hesitated for a moment as if turning over in her mind what Tobin had said to her. Then she shuffled across the bunk and stood up.

'There's a door to the street in the passageway,' she said breathlessly as he hurried her across the room. 'There's stairs behind.'

They pulled open the door and went down the stairs with Tobin holding on to the girl's arm. At the foot of the stairs a short passageway led to the door opening on to the street. Tobin knew that once they stepped outside they'd be risking any one of Masefield's men spotting them. He'd been seen around the town that afternoon but it had been important to act normally. He filled his lungs with air, eased the Colt on his hip and pushed open the door feeling the night air on his face. He half turned to the girl.

'The horses are mebbe twenty yards from here. You OK with that?'

Janey nodded vigorously. 'I just wanna get home.'

Tobin stepped out to the hardpack, the girl maybe two paces behind him. He turned in the direction of the hitching rail where he'd left the two horses and stood quite still. Coming towards him along the edge of the building was the figure of a man. For a moment his face showed in the light thrown from a store on the other side of the street. Joe! The no-good who'd sat with Masefield. Tobin moved quickly to shield Janey but was too late. Joe had closed and recognized them both.

'Hey, Tobin! What the hell—?'

Tobin's razor-sharp throwing knife struck him in the throat, burying itself in the soft skin two inches below his chin. Joe staggered a couple of paces towards them, then blood spurted, and his knees buckled, pitching him forward into the dirt. Wet choking noises came from him, muffled by the soil, before he twitched twice and then was still.

'Oh, my God!' Janey's hand was at her mouth, her eyes wide, pulling away from Tobin as if ready to flee in the opposite direction.

'C'mon, Janey! We gotta get outta here.'

Tobin didn't wait to look – he knew Joe was dead. He strengthened his grip on Janey's arm, dragging her down the street to where the horses stood opposite the closed rear doors of the dry goods store. Fifteen minutes later the horses were splashing through the stream, heading for Bear Creek.

CHAPTER FOUR

A mile out of Bear Creek Tobin reined in his mount and turned in his saddle to look behind him. Janey had halted her horse in the centre of the trail and was lolling in her saddle, her head down.

'You OK, Janey?' Tobin called.

He trotted his mount back a hundred yards, reining in alongside her. Tears were rolling down her face and muffled sobs came from behind the hand at her mouth. He didn't have to think too hard about what was wrong.

'You just made a mistake, Janey. Heck, if I had a dollar for all the mistakes I'd made I'd be a rich man.'

'I thought Frank was—'

'And so, I bet, a passel of gals have thought the same,' he cut in. 'He ain't a bad lookin' feller an' he's got a way about him. But you gotta remember, 'neath all that, he's been ridin' the owlhoot trail all his life and he ain't gonna change now. You'd be runnin' for the rest of your days.'

She lifted her head, and forced a weak smile. 'All the folks in town are gonna think me stupid.'

He shook his head. 'They'll say you've seen sense. You ran off with a wrong 'un, and now you've come home. Your ma's gonna be happy, an' I bet the young bucks in Bear Creek show they're mighty pleased when they see a purty gal like you come back home.'

'The men round these parts only want me cos they know I'm real handy at wagon-drivin'.'

Tobin grinned. 'No, I don't reckon that's it. Mr Devlin wrote me an' said you were the prettiest an' sweetest gal in the county, an' Mr Devlin's real straight.'

'He wrote that? But me an' Frank—' Her voice trailed away and her face coloured.

'An' who's gonna know about that? An' who's gonna care? Most o' the folks in town never even heard o' Frank Masefield. They only know you been away for a coupla weeks.'

'You think folks'll not be tellin'?'

'Sure I do. C'mon Janey, I been seein' that steak in the Chinaman's place since we broke camp.' He held up a hand suddenly as if remembering something. 'I reckon afore we ride into town I'd better show the folks I ain't the no-good they think I am.'

He reached into his saddle-bag, thrusting his hand through the spare shirt and pants nestling at the bottom, and pulled out a silver star which he pinned to his vest. 'Josh Devlin reckoned this might stop me gettin' shot if the Masefields got real ornery.' He grinned. 'I ain't s'posed to wear it in town but it ain't gonna do any harm for a coupla hours.'

He touched his heels to the sides of his mount. 'Let's go, Janey. Time you got into a fancy dress instead of that old slicker.'

The townspeople on the boardwalks stopped to look at Tobin and Janey as they rode down Main Street. There were shouts from some of the men, maybe those who had manned the posse to bring Tobin to the jail. Tobin turned in his saddle making sure that men on both sides of the street could see the star pinned to his vest.

Someone must have alerted Devlin. When Tobin was fifty yards from the sheriff's office Devlin and his deputy appeared at the top of the steps. As Tobin wheeled his mount towards the hitching rail a broad smile broke out on Devlin's face, but the deputy, Charlie Forbes, was frowning.

'What the hell's goin' on here, Sheriff'? An' who's the boy with Tobin?'

Devlin ignored him. 'Hey, Ben,' he called. 'What took you so long?'

'Mebbe we took time out for a picnic!' Tobin said, with a broad grin. He held out a hand to assist Janey to dismount. 'Time this young lady got back to her ma.'

'That's Janey Garner!' Forbes exclaimed as the girl pushed back her hood.

'Come on up here, Janey,' Devlin said. 'I'll get word to your mama, an' we'll get you back to Clearwater.'

'We ain't busy, Mr Devlin,' Forbes said quickly. 'Mebbe I could ride out to Clearwater. If that's fine with you, Miss Janey?'

She gave a shy smile. 'I'd like that, Charlie Forbes.'

'I'll get my horse. When I get back, Mr Devlin, mebbe you'll tell me what's been happenin'. I guess Mr Tobin ain't all he seemed.'

Devlin exchanged an amused glance with Tobin. 'Yeah, good idea, Charlie. You go right ahead. Give me and Mr Tobin here the chance to talk.' He jerked a thumb over his shoulder. 'Coffee's hot, Ben, afore you get cleaned up.'

Forbes took hold of the bridle of Janey's horse while she remounted and they set off down Main Street towards the livery to pick up Forbes's own horse. Devlin and Tobin stepped up to the boardwalk and went into the office. The sheriff took down a couple of tin mugs from hooks pinned to the stucco wall, and poured coffee from the pot standing on the stove.

'Here,' he said, handing Tobin a mug. 'Guess you could use this. You ready to tell me what's been goin' on?'

Tobin took a seat by the desk. 'The local sheriff does what he's told. Frank Masefield's got about twenty men around him and does what he's a mind to. Janey knows she's been foolish but she'll get over it.' Tobin took a mouthful of coffee, frowning at something nagging at him. 'But what's Masefield hangin' around for?'

'It ain't timber money. That gets taken down to Cheyenne.'

'Maybe he's just restin' up.'

Devlin shook his head. 'No, that ain't it. I sure hope he ain't gonna go after the ranch money.' Seeing Tobin's puzzled frown, he explained. 'Ranches in the county bring their money and stuff into Bear Creek every three months, then Pinkerton men come into town and shift it to Cheyenne.'

'Masefield know about that?'

'Yeah, could be. Masefield spent three months here, earlier this year. Just another stranger in town, I reckoned, when I saw him around. That's how he got together with Janey. Didn't cause no trouble. One day he rode out and two weeks later he and his men hit the bank down in Morgantown. We reckoned they'd hightailed it outta the county.' Devlin smiled wryly. 'Frank Masefield got the bank's money. I got his brother.'

'An' now you got Janey back owin' to your smart thinkin'.' Tobin raised his tin mug in salute. 'Bart was forever askin' me about that pocket pistol I stuck in your ribs. He reckoned it

35

came in Miss Summers's apple pie.'

Devlin pulled open the top drawer of his desk. 'Useful little popgun,' he said, holding up the .22 pistol. 'Reminds me o' when we pulled that trick down in Abilene.'

Tobin stood up. 'We'll have a few drinks tonight. I'm gonna get cleaned up, and go callin' afore I get some rest.'

'Keep that badge for a while. Wouldn't want Miss Summers worryin'.'

Tobin grinned. 'Just gonna thank the lady for the pie, that's all.'

'Sure you are. Anyways, I'll be out at the homesteads for a while. Give my regards to Miss Summers. You better get back east afore you find yourself hogtied.'

Tobin waved a dismissive hand in the air and stepped smartly to the street door, leaving Devlin behind him roaring with laughter.

A young girl, no more than fourteen years old, opened the door, her eyes widening as she saw the star on Tobin's vest. She looked up at Tobin and her face screwed up, confusion shadowing her eyes.

'You gonna tell Miss Summers she's got a caller?' Tobin asked gently.

'You ain't our regular deputy,' the girl said, her mouth setting. 'I know Charlie Forbes.'

'No, I ain't. My name's Ben Tobin. But I just bought Janey Garner home to her ma.' He smiled. 'Does that win me any chips?'

The girl nodded slowly. 'Yeah, guess so. I'll tell Miss Summers.'

She turned on her heel and, leaving the door ajar, stepped back into the shadows of the house. Tobin looked after her for a moment, amused by the girl's determination to protect her mistress. A moment later Elizabeth Summers appeared in the doorway, the midday sun highlighting her hair and her smooth pale complexion. She was a fine looking woman, Tobin decided. She looked Tobin fully in the face before her eyes dropped to his silver star.

'Mr Tobin! I don't understand—'

'Sorry, ma'am, for all the play-actin'. Me an' Mr Devlin hatched a plan to get Janey Garner back home. Now that's done I wanted to thank you for the pie you sent. Sure beat the bread an' beans Josh Devlin was givin' me.'

Elizabeth laughed and Tobin thought it was the prettiest laugh he'd ever heard on a woman. Then she said something which surprised him.

'I was about to have coffee, Mr Tobin. Would you care to join me?'

'I sure would,' Tobin said. 'I mean, yes, ma'am, coffee would be fine.'

Elizabeth stepped back, opening the door wider. 'There's a hook for your belt next to my cape,' she said. She walked along the passageway, pausing to speak to the young girl while Tobin unbuckled his gunbelt and hung it with his hat on a stout wooden peg.

'If you'll follow me, Mr Tobin,' Elizabeth said, leading the way, and opening a door at the end of the passage.

They both stepped into a large room which was cool from being away from the rays of the sun. Tobin was immediately struck by the large pianoforte by the window, dominating the end of the room. He'd seen instruments like this back east many times but never in the west. The room was furnished with finer chairs and pictures than he'd expected to see. The drapes at the unusually large window were of fine material bunched with decorated cords. He didn't need to be too smart to know there was money here. Elizabeth indicated a chair and he sat down, thankful that he'd left his spurs behind at the livery stable.

'Janey Garner back home is welcome news. I hope she is well.'

'Yes, ma'am. She wanted to come home to her mama, so I brought her back.'

'I doubt it was that simple.' She smiled, taking any sharpness out of her words. 'Have you known Sheriff Devlin a long time?'

'We met up during the War. Then we both worked for Wells Fargo for a time afore I went back east an' he came out here. He tol' me he had kinfolk round these parts but I think they've all passed on.'

'You must be good friends to come so far to help him.'

'He saved my life a coupla times. We don't talk much about it but I reckon if either of us got into a fix the other'd come runnin'.'

There was a tap on the open door and, at Elizabeth's invitation, the girl who'd first opened the street door to Tobin walked slowly across the room. Her lips pressed together with concentration, the girl put the tray bearing a silver coffee set and delicate china cups and saucers on a small table in front of her mistress.

'Thank you, Millie,' Elizabeth said.

'Yes, ma'am,' she said with a little bob. 'Should I close the door, ma'am?'

Elizabeth's eyes flickered in the direction of Tobin before addressing the young girl. 'You must never ask that, Millie. The door always remains open unless you're told to close it.'

'Yes, ma'am.'

Elizabeth waited until the girl's footsteps went back along the corridor.

'Another year and I'm hoping Millie will be ready for a

grand house in Cheyenne,' she explained. 'I visit friends there regularly. Do you know Cheyenne, Mr Tobin?'

'I'm away there, after sunrise tomorrow,' Tobin said. 'I need to take the railroad back east.'

'You're not tempted to enjoy a few days' rest in Bear Creek?'

'Nothin' would give me more pleasure, ma'am. But I like city life so I'm not plannin' to stay away too long.'

She picked up the small jug. 'Do you take sugar and cream, Mr Tobin?'

'When I can get it, ma'am.'

He leaned forward to take the cup and saucer from her hand and their fingers touched. She looked across at him for a second before dropping her eyes and pulling her own cup and saucer closer to her on the table. Tobin looked around the room.

'That sure is a fine pianoforte, ma'am. After what you tol' me about helping the homesteader's daughter I guess you play very well.'

'Oh, yes, the Ruskin girl. She does appear to have a great gift.'

She looked across at the instrument, the dark wood of its surface beginning to shine as the sun moved around, lighting the room. 'I was lucky to be taught by one of the finest musicians in New York. The people of Bear Creek were astonished that I brought a Steinway pianoforte with me but I couldn't bear to part with it.' She looked up as Tobin got to his feet. 'If you ever return to Bear Creek, Mr Tobin, I'll play for you.'

'I hope that will be possible, ma'am. Now if you'll excuse me I must check on my horse for tomorrow.'

Elizabeth also stood up. 'I'll walk with you to the door.'

*

Tobin had a smile on his face as he walked along Main Street heading for the livery. Some months had passed since he'd sat over china teacups with an attractive woman of his own age. He saw that one of the horses he and Bart Mansfield had taken when they'd broken out of the jail was hitched to the rail outside the dry goods store. Devlin must have returned the animals to the livery with several dollars for the hiring. He reminded himself that he'd need to sell his palomino in Cheyenne before taking the train back east. Then he looked across the street as a shout broke into his thoughts.

'Hey, Tobin!'

A small crowd were gathered around the stagecoach which had passed him as he'd walked down Main Street. He spotted the caller who had stepped away from the knot of people to wave an arm in his direction.

'C'mon over here, Mr Tobin. Somebody you should meet.'

Puzzled, Tobin crossed the street to shake the stranger's outstretched hand. 'Caleb Bolton, range boss outta Clearwater,' he introduced himself. 'Folks been talkin'. Guess you pulled a real smart trick gettin' Janey Garner back home. Always admired that gal, so I'm obliged to you.'

'That cowboy o' yourn. How's he doin'?'

'Damn fool tol' me what he an' Fred were about. I'da shot 'em meself, I caught 'em messin' with Miss Summers. I cut 'em a week's pay, showed what I felt. I sure hope Miss Summers is OK.'

'She's fine,' Tobin said. 'I've just taken coffee with her.'

Bolton looked at him sharply but didn't comment on this latest news. Instead he turned to look back at the passengers disembarking from the stage. 'Come an' meet my boss, if you gonna be around this town.'

Before Tobin could explain that he was leaving the following day Bolton swung on his heel and headed for the stage. Tobin inwardly shrugged; it was easier to follow Bolton. A few words and he'd be free to prepare himself for his journey and get something to eat before meeting up with Josh Devlin in the saloon. He stepped up to the boardwalk as a tall man with silver hair showing beneath his Stetson, stepped down from the stage. His Prince Albert coat was a rich blue, over a patterned vest and a white shirt; the cravat he wore looked like silk. Bolton stepped forward.

'I guess you must be Mr Henry Truman, sir. Welcome to Bear Creek.'

Truman nodded. 'And you must be Mr Bolton. I'm pleased to meet you, sir. People speak highly of you.'

He turned to look at Tobin, glancing at the badge on his vest. 'Ah, the law! Always a welcome sight in these hard times.' He patted at his coat and Tobin saw the outline of what was probably a pocket pistol.

'This is Mr Tobin,' Bolton said. 'He's made sure all is fine out at Clearwater.' Seeing Truman's expression he added, 'Mrs Beth Garner looks after the Big House at the ranch. Her daughter Janey was missin' for a coupla weeks and Mr Tobin's brought her back.'

'Then I'm in your debt, Mr Tobin.' Truman looked around. 'Is that our carriage, Mr Bolton?'

'Yes, sir. Jenkins will drive you out to the ranch. I'll make sure all your boxes follow on.'

'Thank you.' He turned to Tobin. 'Good day, Deputy.'

The two men watched Truman walk along the boardwalk and step down to the street to board the carriage. A flick of the driver's whip a foot above the horse's back sent the carriage moving along the street heading for the trail that led to Clearwater.

'See you around, Tobin,' Bolton said, and turned away to call up to the driver, asking about Truman's boxes.

As Tobin headed for the livery Elizabeth Summers's words came back to him and he regretted not being able to stay in Bear Creek for longer. He'd like to have had more time to talk about old times with Josh. Especially those crazy years they'd spent together in England during the War. It seemed a long time ago, now. Hell, it *was* a long time, some twelve years or more.

He touched the brim of his hat with a finger as one of the townsfolk wished him a good day. They sure were a friendly bunch in town. Getting used to the city again would take a little time. He passed the dry goods store and turned into the alleyway leading to the livery. He knew he'd find his palomino in good shape. The liverymen were ex-cavalry troopers by the name of Wilson who'd both survived the War without a scratch. According to Josh Devlin, the Wilsons reckoned they'd been saved to do the Lord's work with horses.

Tobin stepped through the high wide doors into the shadows of the livery, smelling the tang of horses lined in their stalls on both sides of the barn. Then he stopped suddenly as the metal of a gun barrel ground into his back.

'Drop the gunbelt, Tobin,' a hoarse voice ordered close to his ear. 'You make a wrong move an' you'll die now.'

Slowly, without moving his head, Tobin unbuckled his gunbelt and allowed it to fall to the straw-covered ground. As he did so two figures appeared from the shadows. Both carried sidearms, holding them loosely down by their sides. The taller one, a blue scar showing above his cheekbone, kicked away Tobin's belt.

Tobin had never seen either of the men before. What the hell was going on? Were they Masefield's men? In answer to his question a third figure stepped from the shadows.

'Howdy, Tobin,' Frank Masefield said. 'Guess I missed seein' you coupla nights ago.'

'You'll never get outta town. Devlin's gonna shoot you down soon as you show your face.'

Masefield sighed theatrically. 'The sheriff's out at the homesteads; Forbes is taking Janey to Clearwater.' He shrugged. 'He's welcome to her. She's kinda lacking in some of the finer things in this life.'

'You still ain't gonna make it. You're forgettin' this town's got Volunteers. All of 'em once soldiers.'

'Got to hand it to you, Tobin. You keep on tryin'.' Masefield stepped forward thrusting his face close to Tobin's. 'Bart ain't in the jail, an' he ain't been seen since you and him broke out. Now you got a goddamned star on your vest. What the hell you about?'

Without any warning and before Tobin could raise a hand in defence, Masefield lashed out with a leather-gloved fist. His knuckles slammed into Tobin's face and Tobin's knees buckled. With one swing of his trail boot Masefield kicked Tobin's legs from beneath him, sending him crashing to the ground. Then the three men were on him, kicking and stomping as Tobin attempted to roll himself into a ball, head down, his chin on his chest, his legs pulled up to protect the soft parts of his body. Even as his brain swirled and he felt himself losing consciousness he knew he was wasting his time. They intended to kill him and there was nothing he could do to stop them. Mercifully, blackness filled his mind and he slipped away into a long dark tunnel.

CHAPTER FIVE

Tobin closed the door to his room and walked to the stairs leading down to the lobby of the Majestic Hotel. Halfway down the steps he paused for a moment, clutching at the handrail, feeling the sharp tug of pain at his side. A week flat on his back and a week in a soft chair had put him on the road to recovery but he still had aches and pains. He'd taken Doctor McKenzie's advice and had opted to travel to Cheyenne by the regular stage. The Wilsons, at the livery, had bought the palomino and rig, and Josh Devlin had taken the Winchester off his hands. After a minute the pain in his side eased, and he went down the last few stairs to cross to the desk where the clerk was bent over paperwork. He stood up as Tobin reached the desk.

'Good to see you up an' about, Mr Tobin. You sure are lookin' smart.'

'Mr Harris knows how to dress a man,' Tobin said, mentioning the name of the town's tailor. He smoothed down the lapel of his Prince Albert coat. 'Guess a city suit back east'll not be the same. I'll be takin' the stage tomorrow, so we need to talk about my bill.'

'Sheriff's already settled your bill, Mr Tobin.'

'That's mighty generous of him. Guess he's aimin' to win

44

it back at poker tonight. Then I'll just take my Colt.'

The clerk turned away to take Tobin's gunbelt down from a hook. It was a rule of the hotel that no guest carried a weapon into the hotel and Tobin had no problem in following the routine. Normally, he'd have left his Colt behind when he walked through the town but he was taking no chances. Masefield appeared to have someone in Bear Creek providing information.

Tobin buttoned his coat and walked out into the morning sunlight. The town was busy, the townsfolk going about their business, greeting each other as they passed on the boardwalk; a couple of cowboys rode past heading towards the general store; a carriage passed the hotel. Behind the driver sat an elderly woman holding a parasol to protect her pale complexion against the rays of the early summer sun. The scent of bread being freshly baked reached him, and Tobin breathed in deeply, knowing it was only luck that had kept him alive.

He crossed Main Street intending to see Devlin but his door was shut and the office appeared to be empty. He'd catch Josh later. He walked along the boardwalk touching the brim of his hat to return the greeting of Harris who wished him a good day while looking sharply at his coat. Ten minutes later Tobin was knocking on the door of Elizabeth Summers's house.

'Good morning, Millie,' he greeted the girl.

'Madam's expecting you, Mr Tobin. Please follow me.'

Millie led the way along the corridor. She pushed open the door and Tobin stepped past her into the room. Elizabeth was sitting in the high-backed chair behind the small table where they'd sat taking coffee some two weeks before.

'I'm delighted to see you up and about, Mr Tobin.'

For an instant Tobin thought her reaction was almost worth taking a beating for. There again, maybe not. But it was damnable that he couldn't stay in Bear Creek longer and enjoy more of her company.

'I hope I've not caused any gossip.'

Elizabeth smiled. 'I played music from Monsieur Offenbach at my first town concert.' She raised her eyes to the ceiling in mock horror. 'The ladies thought I was a scarlet woman.' She became serious. 'Doctor McKenzie said you were not to be moved for at least a week.'

Tobin frowned. 'I still don't understand how I came to be here.'

'I'd been to buy eggs when I met Mr Bolton and his two cowboys carrying you. After they'd brought you here we could see you were badly hurt. I sent for Doctor McKenzie who said you were not to be moved. He arranged for the two Harman brothers to nurse you.'

'I must see the Harmans and Bolton again before I leave tomorrow.' Tobin looked across at Elizabeth, as he was beginning to think of her. 'I only wish I could stay longer and be of some service to you.'

She smiled, and paused for a moment before she replied. 'Maybe you can. Would you accompany me on an errand, Mr Tobin?'

'Sure, ma'am.'

'I have to see Mr Wilkins at the bank. It's a matter concerning guns that I don't understand. I'd value your advice.'

Tobin stood up. 'We could meet at the Majestic and walk across to the bank. That will give me time to see the Harmans.'

'Thank you for coming so soon, Miss Summers,' Wilkins said, pushing a chair forward close to the desk. 'Please take a seat.

46

And you, sir.'

For a small town banker Wilkins's office showed signs of money having been spent. His mahogany desk sported fancy carvings, there were pots of flowers on shelves, and an original painting on the wall by a window. A smile appeared on Wilkins's face and Tobin guessed that the banker had noticed his appraisal of the office.

'The bank is fortunate to have the backing of the New Amsterdam Company. They also own Clearwater, as you may know.'

Tobin acknowledged the banker's remarks with a nod of his head. But what had caught his particular attention was the huge safe standing against the far wall. The dull metal front was broken only by three brass knobs and a curved brass handle. Tobin hadn't seen a safe like that since he'd left Pittsburgh.

The banker gestured to a chair for Tobin and took his own behind the desk before adjusting his spectacles and shuffling the papers in front of him. Then he cleared his throat and looked directly at Elizabeth Summers.

'Your late brother-in-law Mr Finney, the gunsmith, was owed a large amount of money at his death. That money should now come to you as his sole heir.' His lips twitched briefly. 'I'm aware, of course, that you have independent means but, nevertheless, Mr Finney's affairs cannot be settled until this money is paid.'

'My brother-in-law and I did not enjoy harmonious relations, Mr Wilkins. I was not happy with how he cared for my late sister. If it's a question of disposing of the money you may give it to the poor of the town.'

'That is most generous but I'm afraid it's not that simple, Miss Summers. You are his legal heir, and only after all debts are settled can you can decide what to do with the money.'

Elizabeth Summers looked thoughtful. 'You spoke of guns last week, Mr Wilkins. Who owes the money and what was bought?'

'The Clearwater Ranch purchased a number of Winchester rifles from Mr Finney only a week before his tragic accident.'

Elizabeth Summers turned to Tobin. 'My brother-in-law was killed when his carriage overturned five miles south of the town,' she explained.

'Does it give any details of the long guns?' Tobin asked Wilkins.

Wilkins ran a finger down the paper. 'Fifty long guns made by the Winchester Company but that's all.' He looked up to see Tobin push his lips together in a silent whistle. 'You appear surprised, Mr Tobin.'

'I sure am. I'm wonderin' why cattlemen would need so many long guns.' He looked at Elizabeth. 'I saw Bolton go into the saloon as we walked up here. I need to see him. Why don't I walk over now and ask him about the Winchesters? He should have the answer.'

'Yes. We could meet again in the Majestic for coffee.'

Tobin got to his feet. 'Then I'll bid you good day, Mr Wilkins.' He picked up his hat from the table and left the room as the banker began to explain the process of other monies being paid to Elizabeth's credit.

Bolton was sitting with his back to the batwing doors when Tobin entered the saloon. He walked across to the bar and pointed to the bottle of whiskey set apart from the other bottles.

'I'll take that bottle,' he said, taking a couple of bills from an inside pocket of his Prince Albert.

The barkeep raised an eyebrow. 'That ain't cheap whiskey you're choosin'.'

'That's why I'm takin' it.' Tobin pushed the bills across the bar. 'An' I'll need a glass.'

He picked up the bottle the barkeep put on the bar and, carrying the glass, he walked across the sawdust-covered floor to where Bolton sat talking with a couple of his cowboys. Bolton looked up as Tobin reached the table.

'Guess I don't need to ask how you're keepin'. You in that fancy coat, an' all.' He turned to the cowboys. 'OK boys. I'll see you back at Clearwater. Me an' Mr Tobin are gonna have a talk.'

The two men got to their feet and with nods in Tobin's direction headed for the door. Tobin held up the bottle.

'I guess I owe you more than a few drinks.'

Bolton shrugged. 'Me an' a coupla o' the boys just happened along at the right time. Seems those no-goods didn't want to be seen. Anyways, who were they?'

'The fancy dressed feller was Frank Masefield. Janey Garner was with him when I found her.'

Bolton swore. 'Goddamnit. I'da known that I'd have put a bullet in him.' He looked at the bottle Tobin had put on the table. 'You gonna open that?'

'I sure am.'

He uncorked the bottle and poured them each a generous shot. They lifted their glasses in a silent toast, both of them drinking the whiskey down in one gulp. Tobin poured two more drinks.

Bolton blew air out through pursed lips. 'Hell! That's good whiskey.'

'The bottle's yourn. Those no-goods woulda killed me had you not come along. If there's anything else I can do for you, just say so.' Bolton shrugged but remained silent. 'I gotta question for you,' Tobin continued. 'Clearwater bought fifty Winchesters from the gunsmith Finney. I'm told at the bank they haven't been paid for. I thought you might know something about it.'

Bolton grinned. 'You sure get around, Tobin. Finney was kinfolk o' Miss Summers. I hope you ain't plannin' on takin' her back east.' His grin faded. 'But I ain't heard nothin' of Winchesters. Finney came out once a year havin' a look at the guns we got 'round the ranch. We bought a coupla scatterguns a coupla months back. But that's all.' He paused for a moment. 'What the hell would we do with fifty Winchesters? That's enough for an army.'

'I've been thinkin' the same. But it's all down in Finney's book. I'm told he wasn't the most agreeable of men but he was a good businessman.'

Bolton nodded. 'He was a nasty sonovabitch but he knew his guns. Anyways, I'll check when I get back an' let Wilkins know what I come up with.'

Tobin was about to reply when both men turned towards the door as the jingling of spurs and the thud of boots on wooden boards sounded throughout the saloon.

'Mr Tobin!'

Charlie Forbes stood ten feet into the saloon, his face as white as a linen sheet. For a moment, words spilled out of his mouth making little sense. Then he swallowed noisily still staring at the two men.

'You gotta come to the office, Mr Tobin! Fast as you can make it.'

Tobin stood in the doorway of the sheriff's office and reached behind him to close the door to the street. Not for a second did he take his eyes off the figure of Devlin slumped back in his seat behind the desk. To Tobin his friend could have been dozing after too many whiskeys save for the dark trickle of blood that stained the side of his head and was now congealing on his high cheekbone.

'Why the hell would he do somethin' like this?' Forbes burst out.

Tobin didn't reply. Instead he walked to the side of the desk to look down at the .22 pistol that lay on the rough matting. Devlin's arm hung slackly down and the pistol was maybe four or five inches away from his fingers.

'How long since you found him?'

'No more than a few minutes. We'd been out at the homesteads. On our way back the sheriff said he had to call on Clearwater. I guessed he was callin' on Janey's ma.'

'So what did you do?'

'I came straight back to town an' I stopped off at the general store. I put my horse in the livery barn then spent an hour or two walkin' the town makin' sure that it was quiet. Then I was mebbe half an hour talkin' to the councilman who owns the hardware store afore I walked back here. That's when I found the sheriff like this.'

'Was he dead when you got here?'

Forbes swallowed. 'He was alive for mebbe a moment or two. He reached up and grabbed me an' tried to say somethin'.'

'What was it?'

Forbes chewed at his lip. 'I ain't really sure. I think he said "Deadwood" or "Deadline", somethin' like that.'

'Deadline mean anythin' to you?'

'I know what the sheriff's deadline is. We cross over our thirty-two square miles an' the badge means nothin'.'

Tobin thought for a moment. Deadwood was a town to the north east. Aside from what Forbes had just explained, the expression deadline meant nothing to him. A head wound could have caused Josh to say almost anything. What was said need not have meant anything at all. But why would his old

51

friend kill himself? Could he have been mortally ill and reckoned this was the best way out? But if that was the case,
choosing the office for his final moments was mighty strange.

'He ever talk about the slug in his back?'

Forbes frowned. 'What you talkin' about?'

'We were both workin' for Wells Fargo a few years back.
Some no-goods were plannin' to hit a bank, an' we were
waitin' for 'em. There was a shoot-out an' Josh took a slug in
his back. The surgeon's said it was too close to his spine to
move it.'

'You mean he's been walkin' round these years with it in
him?'

'The surgeons tol' him if it ever shifted he'd not be able to
lift a finger. Mebbe the time had come. How's he been these
last weeks?'

'Mr Devlin was an even-minded feller. He used to get a
mite down after he'd seen Janey's ma. I reckon the sheriff
wanted to marry her an' Beth Garner wouldn't have him. But
a coupla days and he'd be himself agin.'

'He been callin' on Doc McKenzie?'

Forbes shook his head. 'He ain't never said that.'

'What took you to the homesteads this morning?'

'Collectin' taxes but we get no hassle out there.'

'An' before you went collectin' taxes?'

'Mayor Parker brought that Mr Truman from Clearwater
to meet the sheriff, so Mr Devlin tol' me. Mr Truman was
keen to meet as many folks as he could afore he went back to
the ranch.'

'Anyone else been around? How about Skippy?'

'Skippy's been sick for a coupla days, holed up in his
cabin. I didna come in the office first thing. I met the sheriff
at the livery.' Forbes frowned. 'Sheriff did say somethin'
about long guns. Said he'd need to look into it.'

Tobin thought for a moment. 'Go get whoever takes care o' the dead, an' tell him to keep his mouth shut about how Josh died. Ask Doc McKenzie if the sheriff was ill or anythin', then get the mayor over here. I'll be back in ten minutes or so.'

Tobin left the office and crossed Main Street to take the steps to the Majestic two at a time. Without stopping to drop off his gunbelt with the clerk he strode along the passageway to the small parlour where he knew Elizabeth would be waiting. She looked up, a little startled at his sudden appearance in the doorway.

'Is anything wrong?'

Tobin took the seat opposite her. 'Sheriff Devlin's dead,' he said abruptly.

Her hand went to her mouth. 'Oh, my goodness! Was it an accident?'

Tobin shook his head. 'Seems he shot himself. But we're keepin' quiet about that.'

'The poor man. Why would he do such a terrible thing?'

'I don't know.' He leaned forward. 'When I was settlin' with the Harmans were you sitting here all the time?'

'Yes, I was.'

Tobin turned and looked towards the window. He stood up and moved to stand behind Elizabeth's chair. Then he ducked his head until he was at her level. Through the window he could see directly to the door of the sheriff's office.

'Josh Devlin was in his office alone after he an' the deputy came back from the homesteads.' He stood up. 'Did you see anyone going in?'

She thought for a moment, half turning in her chair to look up at him before shaking her head. 'Nobody went in while I was here. No, wait! Mrs Garner, Janey Garner's mother called.'

'I'm sorry I can't walk you home but I have to get back. I hope there'll be other times.'

'I hope you return to Bear Creek soon, Mr Tobin.'

'I'm not leavin' yet, ma'am. There's somethin' goin' on I need to get a handle on.'

'Henry Parker, Mr Tobin,' the mayor of Bear Creek introduced himself. He shook Tobin's hand warmly. 'We shall miss Josh Devlin. He was a good man. It's a sad business when anyone dies, no matter how. More so with Josh. He was well thought of by all the townsfolk. Always dressed so well, somethin' that sits kindly on a man.'

Forbes brought across a chair for the mayor, and to Tobin's surprise gestured that he, Tobin, should take the chair behind the desk. He looked at Forbes to check that he'd understood correctly, and seeing Forbes's nod, moved behind the desk. When all three men were seated Parker took from his pocket a sheet of paper.

'I have here the signatures of the councilmen,' he said. 'We can nominate a sheriff while we organize a new election. That will take time and the town needs lawmen.' He replaced the paper in a pocket of his coat. 'Josh let me in on his plan to bring back Janey Garner. He thought you brave and he trusted you, Mr Tobin. That means I trust you.' He put his hands firmly on the desk. 'Will you be our sheriff until the election?'

Tobin didn't reply immediately. Then he shook his head.

'No, Mr Parker, I thank you for your offer but I can't do that. I'm gonna stick around for a while but I need to get back east. I've a better notion. Charlie here is an able man. Make him sheriff, an' that gives him a chance at the election. I'll serve as his deputy for a while. Help out when he needs it.'

Parker turned to Forbes. 'How you gonna be, givin' orders to a man like Mr Tobin?'

'I'm sure we'd make a good team, Mr Parker.'

The mayor laughed loudly. 'A politician already, Charlie! Good for you!' He turned back to Tobin. 'You should know the town don't pay much for a deputy.'

'I can't take your money, Mr Parker. Spend it on the schoolhouse or somethin'.'

Parker stood up, as did the other two men. 'That's mighty generous. Are you sure about that?'

'I'm sure.'

'Then it's agreed.' He stuck a hand out to Tobin who grasped it firmly. 'I bid you good day, gentlemen.'

As he reached the door it was opened from the street by a small man with a shock of white hair. He was dressed in black, save for a crisp white shirt, against which a black four-in-hand showed below his stiff collar. He greeted the mayor and stood aside to allow him to pass.

'Shut the door, Jed,' Forbes said to the new arrival. 'You find a letter or anythin' on Mr Devlin?'

'No letter,' said Jed, who Tobin assumed was the town's undertaker. 'A few coins, two dollar bills and a timepiece was all he was carryin' in his pockets. They're under lock and key across my parlour. There was this, though,' he continued.

He took from his pocket a square of what Tobin at first thought was paper. The undertaker put it on the desk and Tobin saw that it was a picture of a Union soldier in uniform. Behind the man's head was a light vertical stripe, probably on another uniform and Tobin guessed that the picture had been cut from one similar to those favoured by the famous photographer Matthew Brady during the War.

'I'll collect the sheriff's stuff later, Jed,' Forbes said. 'We'll keep this for a while.'

'Jed, I've remembered somethin',' Tobin said. 'You didn't find a little medal Mr Devlin carried. Had a picture of a saint on it I recall.'

'Yeah, I remember that now, real silver I reckon,' Forbes said.

The undertaker shook his head. 'Nothin' like that.' He turned towards the door. 'I'll be in the parlour when you need me.'

When they were alone Tobin looked at Forbes. 'That feller Jed. Is he honest?'

'Sure is. If you're thinkin' o' Mr Devlin's medal, it ain't there. I'd stake my last dollar on it.'

Tobin nodded. 'OK, let's take another look at that picture.'

Both men bent over the desk to examine the photograph. 'Mebbe this is Mr Devlin's brother,' suggested Forbes. 'I heard he was killed in the War.'

'Yeah, at Andersonville.'

'That a town?'

Tobin shook his head. 'Johnny Reb prison camp. A lot o' good men died there.' He blew silently through pursed lips, pushing the picture with one finger a few inches across the desk into the brighter light. 'This picture coulda been made ten years ago or more,' he said slowly. 'Am I crazy or could this be Truman who's come to Clearwater?'

Forbes looked at the picture for a long moment. 'I ain't sure I agree with that,' he said slowly. He looked straight at Tobin. 'But just lookin' at you I got the sudden notion that this is gonna get real dirty.' He turned on his heel and walked over to a shelf and took down a Bible. 'I know you got that star Mr Devlin gave you but now you're a proper deputy you gotta take an oath or it ain't legal.'

CHAPTER SIX

Tobin had covered maybe five hundred yards from the sign swinging from chains that marked the boundary of Clearwater when a rider emerged from the cover of the cottonwoods. Tobin slowed his palomino to a walk, waiting for the rider to approach him. Was it just happenstance the rider had been around or was he there to check on strangers? He was no cowboy that was for sure. Not with a Frontier Colt on his belt.

'Deputy Tobin, callin' on Mr Truman,' Tobin said, as the rider reined in a few yards away.

'An' why you doin' that?'

'If Mr Truman wants you to know, he'll tell you.'

The rider pulled his lips back on to his teeth. 'You bein' smart?'

Tobin rested his hands on the pommel of his saddle. What was going on here? All ranches guarded their territory from interlopers but he'd arrived peacefully and wearing a badge and he was surprised Bolton would hire someone who shot off his mouth in front of the law. With the ease of much practice Tobin drew his Navy and with a rigid arm pointed it at the man.

'This is bein' smart. I shoot you now, I reckon folks'll

57

believe any story I wanna tell 'em.'

Colour drained from the man's face. 'Jesus Christ! I was only askin'!'

'Next time have some manners. Now turn 'round an' ride back into those cottonwoods. I see you agin an' I'm gonna haul you back to jail. You got that?'

The rider nodded, his face damp with sweat. There was a click as Tobin cocked the Navy.

'Then say it.'

'I got it, mister! I got it!'

Tobin eased the hammer back and lowered the Navy as he watched the rider turn his mount's head and kick the animal forward into a trot heading for the stand of cottonwoods. Tobin muttered a curse. What the hell was wrong with him? Sure, that no-good needed to be told. But threatening to shoot him was crazy. Maybe Josh Devlin's death had affected him more than he cared to admit. He dropped his sidearm into its holster, touched the sides of his palomino, and took the track leading to the Big House of the Clearwater ranch. He'd need to control his temper when talking with Truman.

'Hey, Tobin! I thought you was quittin' Bear Creek. An' I see you got your palomino back.'

Bolton called out as he descended the wide steps from the main door of the Big House. As Tobin dismounted Bolton said something to the young boy alongside him who promptly ran down the steps to take the palomino's bridle and lead it to a hitching rail.

'Cost me twenty dollars more than the Wilsons at the livery paid me on the first deal.' Tobin shrugged. 'I still reckon I did OK.' He looked at Bolton as the range boss stepped down from the last step to the hardpack in front of the house. 'Saw one o' your men a while back. Kinda rough sorta *hombre*.'

Bolton shook his head. 'He ain't one o' mine. Mine are all out with the beef. That feller you saw rode in last night, tol' me he'd been hired by Mr Truman.'

'You any notion why?'

Bolton frowned. 'You askin' these questions 'cos you got that badge on your vest?'

'That's about it. So what about this new man?'

'Mr Truman said he'll explain in a while.' Bolton shrugged. 'The feller ain't gonna mess with the beef, so to hell with him.'

'I came to see your boss but first I wanna ask you something.'

'I hope this ain't gonna take a lotta time. Mr Truman's gonna spend a coupla hours with me. An' we got work to do.'

'You call on the sheriff anytime this mornin'?'

'Yeah, I was in town mebbe an hour after sunup.'

'What did you talk about?'

'For Christ's sake, Tobin. Why not ask Devlin yourself?'

Tobin looked at Bolton carefully. Was the range boss play-acting or did he really not know Josh Devlin was dead? If he'd ridden out of town from the saloon it was very possible. If he'd been involved in the sheriff's death something must have surely shown on his face.

'Josh Devlin was found dead in his office earlier today.'

Bolton pursed his lips in a silent whistle. 'Hell! That's hard. He wasn't fifty, I bet. How'd he die?'

'Heart gave out,' Tobin said. It was the truth more or less. 'You gonna tell me what you talked about?'

'Some sonovabitch is runnin' off our cattle. Mebbe jest one or two. If we hadna been doing a count of stock we probably wouldna noticed.'

'Any notion who might be rustlin'?'

Bolton shook his head. 'I was askin' if any strangers had

come into town. A coupla fancy drummers from Cheyenne sellin' clothes for the ladies. I reckon they ain't gonna be stealin' our beef.'

'OK, me and Charlie Forbes'll keep a lookout. Now I need to see your boss.'

'I'm here, Mr Tobin.'

Tobin looked up to the door: framed in the doorway was the figure of Henry Truman. Instead of the Prince Albert and the silk vest in which he'd arrived at Bear Creek he was dressed in trail clothes.

'What brings you out here, Deputy?'

'I got a few questions, Mr Truman,' Tobin replied. 'I guess you're busy but I gotta ask you to give me some of your time.'

Truman nodded. 'You go ahead, Bolton. I'll be along in a while.' He turned back to Tobin. 'Follow me.'

The two men went across a wide hall and into a room which appeared to have been set up as an office for Truman. A large desk occupied the space in front of a window which threw light on to an untidy pile of papers. Behind the desk was a high-backed chair and in front stood two plain wooden chairs a couple of feet apart. Truman waved Tobin to take one, and moved to take his own seat behind the desk.

'Fire away, Deputy,' he said, when both of them were seated.

'Does Deadwood mean anything to you?'

'Town in the Black Hills. Couple of Custer's soldiers found gold a couple of years back. Started a gold rush.'

'That's all?'

'What more do you want, Deputy?'

'How about Deadline?'

Did Truman's eyes flicker with recognition? Tobin wasn't sure. He looked hard at Truman who appeared to be thinking about the question. Truman shook his head.

'Means nothing to me.'

Tobin nodded. 'You mind tellin' me why you came to Clearwater right now? Why not last month or mebbe later this year?'

Truman twisted his mouth. 'The Company likes to protect its interests. Bolton's a good man but our trust only goes so far.'

'You ever serve in the army, Mr Truman?'

Truman raised an eyebrow at the sudden switch in topic. 'What a strange question. Yes, in the War I was with the 15th Massachusetts. We took a helluva beating at Ball's Bluff.'

Truman hesitated and for a second Tobin thought he was going to add to his statement but the moment passed. He reached into the pocket of his vest and pulled out the photograph of the Union soldier and placed it on the desk. Did Truman's eyes flicker with a sign of recognition? Again Tobin wasn't sure.

'A fine set of moustaches,' remarked Truman after a pause to examine the photograph, 'although I've never been tempted to grow them myself.' He looked up at Tobin. 'You mind telling me what this is all about? I'm a busy man, Deputy, and these questions are beginning to waste my time.'

'Sheriff Devlin died in his office this morning.'

Truman's lips tightened. 'I'm sorry to hear that. He didn't look ill when I saw him with the mayor.' He frowned. 'But what's his death got to do with this?' He tapped the photograph with a neatly trimmed fingernail.

'It was found in Josh Devlin's pocket.'

'So why have you brought it to me?'

'You could be that soldier mebbe ten, twelve years ago.'

'You're out of your mind, Deputy.' Truman stood up, his expression showing his irritation. 'I've helped as much as I can,' he said abruptly. 'Bolton will be waiting for me.' He walked to the door looking straight ahead as if Tobin didn't exist.

'That mebbe wasn't my smartest move,' Tobin admitted grimly as he dangled the mug of coffee on his knee. His mouth twitched. 'You take that as your first lesson, Charlie. Use your brains an' think hard afore you make a move.'

'You still reckon Truman's the soldier in the picture?'

Tobin took his boot off the desk and pushed his chair forward. 'I ain't sure now, Charlie. Truman came over as tellin' the truth, and men in uniform with moustaches can look the same.'

The two men looked to the door as Jed Barrett, the town's undertaker, stepped into the office, a pile of clothes in his arms, a pair of leather boots clutched in one hand.

'Thought I'd better bring these over, Mr Forbes, afore we plant the sheriff tomorrow. These are mighty fine clothes. It ain't right that Josh Devlin's stuff gets thrown away.'

'Thanks, Jed. Put 'em on the table 'cross there,' Forbes said. 'You still ain't found a letter or anythin'?'

'No, sir. Pockets all empty. Just the stuff I already brung.'

'OK, Jed. Thanks fer your time. I'll be settlin' any bills.'

There was silence in the office for a few moments after the undertaker had left the office. Finally, with a deep intake of breath, Forbes got to his feet and crossed to where the clothes sat piled on the table.

'S'pose I could give 'em to a coupla the town's poor,' Forbes said. 'But I got a hankerin' after the leather vest.'

'I'm sure Josh woulda been pleased,' Tobin said.

Forbes sorted through the clothing until he came up with the vest and held it up to examine it. Then he slipped off his own leather vest to shrug his shoulders into the fine garment.

'Looks good on you, Charlie.'

'It sure fits easy,' Forbes said. 'I reckon I'll keep it on.'

'Hold on, Charlie,' Tobin said. 'What's that stain on the side?'

Forbes looked down, twisting his neck to see what Tobin was pointing at. Unable to see for himself, Forbes slipped off the vest and brought it back to the desk so the two men could get a better look.

'Jesus!' Forbes exclaimed. 'I think that's blood! But how the hell could blood get on that side of the vest?'

'Hold on, Charlie,' Tobin said. He picked up the vest and held it close to his nose. 'That ain't blood, that's some sorta juice from fruit.' He frowned, thinking over what Forbes had told him about his and Josh's movements on the day of Devlin's death. 'Did I see Janey's ma about town today?'

Forbes nodded. 'Saw her meself through the window mebbe ten minutes ago.'

'Go find her. I gotta coupla questions.'

Tobin was finishing his coffee when Forbes returned accompanied by Beth Garner. She was dressed in a plain blue cotton dress partly covered by a clean white apron. Her features were strong and she met Tobin's gaze unflinching although her eyelids were red and her eyes bloodshot. Tobin guessed she'd spent some while in tears during the last few days.

'Take a seat, Mrs Garner. I've a coupla questions.' He paused while the woman settled herself into the chair. 'I have to talk 'bout you an' Josh.'

As if the dead sheriff's name released a spring within her, the woman's hand shot from beneath her apron to re-emerge clutching a square of white linen with which she dabbed at her swollen eyes. For a few moments her head was down, her eyes fixed on a point in the middle of her apron. Then she looked up at Tobin.

'Such a fine man,' she said, her voice near breaking point. 'I wanted to thank you both together for returning Janey to me.'

'On the day Josh died did you see him?'

She shook her head.

'So you didn't come back with him from Clearwater?'

She frowned. 'No, I was already in town.'

Tobin exchanged glances with Forbes. 'I ain't sure I'm followin' you.'

'Once a month I spend a couple of days in town to fix things for the ranch,' she explained. 'I get ribbons an' stuff, buy pans at the General Store, visit Mr Wilkins at the bank, do all the business I need to for the Clearwater House.'

'So when did you see Josh Devlin last?'

She looked away from him, staring hard at the window overlooking Main Street. Her lips were set in a firm line, and after a moment she screwed her eyes tightly closed.

'Mrs Garner, you were seen to come to this office on the morning that Josh Devlin died. I cain't believe you had a hand in his death but I must find out as much as I can what happened that morning. Now look this way an' I'll ask you agin,' Tobin said, his voice harsh. 'When did you last see Josh Devlin?'

Beth Garner turned her head to face him. To Tobin's surprise, her face was scarlet. Her head went down and she plucked nervously at the edge of her apron. Across the office, Forbes looked at Tobin, a slight curve to his lips.

'Mrs Garner,' Forbes said. 'I happen to know that every month Mr Devlin took a room for a coupla nights at the Majestic. He used to say he needed a change from the old shack where he lived.' He paused, and added softly. 'Nothin's gonna be said outside this office.'

The woman's head jerked around to look at both Tobin

and Forbes in turn. 'Yes, all right. I was with Josh Devlin the night before he died.' She sat up straight in the chair, her shoulders back. 'An' I'm proud of it. He was a fine man.'

'He was a fine man, Mrs Garner,' Tobin agreed, his voice softer. 'I was glad to call him my friend. Thank you for comin' in.'

Her defiant attitude disappeared as quickly as it had registered on the set of her face. She looked at both of them in turn. 'May I go now?'

'One more question,' Tobin said. He held up the leather vest Devlin had worn. 'Did you see this stain the night you were with him?'

The shadow across her eyes showed that she'd recognized immediately to whom the vest had once belonged. She shook her head. 'Josh wouldn't walk a yard with that on his vest.' Her nose wrinkled. 'That's blueberry, I reckon.' Again she shook her head, obviously puzzled. 'We're making jelly back at the House, but how come it's got on to Josh?'

'I don't know, Mrs Garner,' Tobin said grimly. 'But I aim to find out.'

CHAPTER SEVEN

Tobin held the reins lightly allowing the pony to keep its own pace as the buggy rolled along the track heading east from Bear Creek. From where he and Elizabeth sat alongside each other Tobin couldn't see the lake they were heading for but he reckoned that it was no more than a couple of miles away.

'Mebbe I shoulda brought a fish pole, an' I coulda caught your supper.'

Elizabeth smiled. 'I can't see you with a fish pole, Mr Tobin.'

'Now there you've got me all wrong,' Tobin said as he flicked the reins above the back of the pony, the buggy's wheels throwing up dust from the dry track. 'I learned to catch fish when I was in England during the War.'

'You weren't in the army?'

'I was for a year. Then Mr Pinkerton who worked for President Lincoln sent me to London. That's when I first met Josh Devlin. We spent three years together diggin' out facts an' figures on cargoes being shipped to the Confederacy.' Tobin shrugged. 'I ain't sure we did much good.' He spoke quickly before Elizabeth could reply. 'How's that young gal of yourn at the pianoforte?'

'Emma Ruskin? She really needs to go back east. She's worthy of better facilities than I can provide here.'

'I guess you must be a fine player to know that.'

'I *was* a fine player,' Elizabeth said slowly, and Tobin

looked around at her, detecting a note of regret. 'Forgive me, that was immodest,' she said. 'I was fortunate to have a wonderful teacher—' She broke off as Tobin bent suddenly to grab his Colt from beneath the bench seat.

'What's wrong?'

'Edge of the trail by those cottonwoods. There's a horse and a man on the ground.'

'Oh, my God! I can see them now.'

'It's probably nothin'. The man might be sleepin'. But the horse on the ground troubles me. You OK we take a look?'

Her face set, Elizabeth nodded. In response Tobin turned the pony's head off the trail and sent the buggy rocking and bumping across the uneven meadow until they were a few yards away from the animal on the ground. Tobin halted the buggy and stepped down, his Navy held loosely down by his side. Close up he could see bone protruding through the flesh of the horse's leg. The animal must have been struggling to stand, its flesh lathered in sweat, as it lay exhausted, its head covered in flies. Tobin turned back to Elizabeth.

'Look away,' he ordered.

Not waiting for an answer he turned back, raised his Navy, and put the animal out its misery, the sound of the shot bouncing off the nearby stand of trees. He waited until he was sure the animal was dead, meanwhile staring at the saddle with its decorated pommel, something tugging at the back of his mind. He shook his head, exasperated, unable for the moment to dig it from his memory. Maybe it would come to him. He walked over to the body of the man on the ground, knowing there was no need to hurry. The angle of the man's neck told Tobin the man had been killed instantly when thrown from his horse.

'Is he alive?' Elizabeth called.

'No, 'fraid not. We'll get somebody from town come an' pick him up.'

He bent and slid the man's sidearm from its holster and was surprised to recognize a .36 Savage Navy Revolver. A lot of gun for an honest citizen. This *hombre* might have kept company with the rider he'd come across at Clearwater. Tobin whirled around suddenly, startling Elizabeth who had been looking his way.

'What's wrong?' Elizabeth asked.

'I've jest remembered. This no-good's from Ellistown. I recall seein' the saddle there with its fancy pommel.' Tobin walked back to the carcass of the dead horse, pulled the long gun from its scabbard and examined it carefully. He stood for a minute thinking about what he'd found then turned to walk back to the buggy. Masefield must have been planning something for a very long time. But what the hell was it?

'Sorry about the picnic. We need to get back to town,' he called to Elizabeth.

'Take a look, an' tell me what you got.'

Tobin held out to Forbes the long gun he'd taken from the scabbard of the dead man he and Elizabeth had come across during their buggy ride. While Forbes examined the long gun Tobin walked across the office and poured himself coffee from the pot standing on the iron stove.

'It don't take much brains to know it's a Winchester,' Forbes said. 'But I ain't seen nothing like this one afore.'

'It's a '76 model. One of a thousand. An' I reckon Masefield's got fifty of 'em, or mebbe I should say forty-nine, now we got that one.'

'Jumpin' rattlesnakes! How'd they get hold of 'em? They must cost plenty o' dollars.'

'Thirty-five dollars each, but Masefield didn't buy 'em. I reckon there was a deal worked through Finney the gunsmith using Clearwater's name.'

'You tellin' me Caleb Bolton an' Masefield are in cahoots?'

'I ain't sure, but somethin's goin' on out there.'

'Mebbe Masefield's gonna hit the Morgantown bank agin.' Forbes stopped suddenly, his face grim. 'Christ! Our bank!'

Tobin shook his head. 'They must be thinkin' o' somethin' else, somethin' a lot bigger. No-goods like Masefield don't need fifty '76 Winchesters to take a small town bank.'

Forbes smacked his open hand against his forehead. 'Hell! The ranch money.'

Tobin thought for a moment. 'How long we got afore the ranches bring in the money?'

'Came in this mornin'. I've been over with Wilkins.'

'Mebbe that's why Truman's here.'

Both men looked up as the street door opened and a tall elderly man wearing bib coveralls and a greasy-looking hat stepped into the office.

'You lookin' for me, Zack?' Forbes asked.

'I'm darned sure I'm lookin' for somebody.'

'What's the problem?' Tobin asked.

'Miss Summers hired me to clear out Mr Finney's workshop.'

Forbes sat up suddenly. 'You ain't found any weapons still there? Sheriff Devlin had the place cleared out.'

'Then the sheriff didna find the room below the floor. Cos there's a gun down there bigger than I've ever seen in my life.'

'What sorta gun?'

'Hell, I don't know.'

'You tol' Miss Summers?'

Zack shook his head. 'The lady's gone out to the homesteads. Teachin' some gal the peeyanna, if I recall right.'

Tobin and Forbes got to their feet. 'OK, Zack,' Tobin said. 'You go back there and we'll be along an' take a look.' Tobin waited until they were alone before he asked the question. 'What sort of a feller was Finney?'

'He was a good gunsmith, I'll give him that. But he was an ornery sort. He didn't look after his wife like a man should.'

'She was Miss Summers's sister?'

'Yeah, that's right. I heard that his wife wasn't cold in the ground afore he was tryin' to cozy up to Miss Summers. But she weren't having any of it.

'I heard Finney got hisself killed in a buggy spill.'

'That's what folks said.'

Tobin looked at him sharply. 'You got other notions?'

'There was talk of him selling guns to a bunch o' renegade Shoshone holed up some fifty miles from here. But nothin' was ever proved. When we found him Mr Devlin saw the hole in Finney's head an' thought it coulda come from an axe, but the judge decided different.'

'No gunsmith moved in to take Finney's place?'

'Town don't need one. Finney was strugglin' to make a livin'. Mebbe that's how he got into sellin' guns to the Shoshone. Feller who bought the general store about the same time as Finney was killed, name o' Bradden, saw his chance and said he'd stock enough guns for Bear Creek.'

'OK, let's take a look at Finney's place.'

The two men went down to the street, crossing to the other side to where an alley cut between the livery and the saloon. At the end of the alleyway a single clapboard building stood beneath a couple of trees. Zack was standing at the doorway waiting for them; he took out a large brass key and unlocked the door. In the shadowy space inside, a bench at waist height ran around three walls, its oil-stained surface bare except for an oil lamp and shards of metal which Tobin guessed were the remains of the gunsmith's work.

Zack kicked aside a lumpy rope mat which lay on the ground in the centre of the workshop. Loose boards had been pulled aside to show wooden steps leading down to a cellar below the floor. Forbes took out a match and lit the lamp on the bench. When it had burned long enough to throw sufficient light he passed it over to Tobin who lowered his shoulders to avoid cracking his head, and felt his way down the steps with Forbes following him.

At the end of the cellar straw was scattered around a large wooden crate. As Tobin reached the crate he could see that Zack must have removed only a couple of planks from the top of the crate, but it was enough for him to see the blue metal glint by the light of the lamp.

'Zack, you got an iron bar or somethin'?' Forbes called.

There was the clank of metal against metal before Zack handed down a bar to Forbes who had retreated to the steps. Forbes swore loudly as he banged his head on the low timbers as he came back to hand the iron bar to Tobin. A few minutes later the remaining wood of the top of the crate had been removed and the top layers of straw tossed aside.

'Fer Chris'sakes! What we got here?'

Tobin rested a hand on the metal of the barrel nestling in straw. How the hell did this ever end up in a small town gun-smith's workshop? Was there more to Finney than anyone in the town had realized?

'Charlie, we're gonna have to talk to Cap'n Wallace. Mebbe one of his Volunteers can handle this. If this sonov-abitch works OK, Masefield's gonna wonder what the hell hit 'em when they try an' take the bank.'

'Come in, Mr Tobin, come in.'

The ex-army captain, a vigorous 50-year-old, stood in the doorway of his clapboard. His grey beard reached the 'V' of his leather vest beneath a rough blue cotton jacket. From his mouth jutted a white clay pipe which bubbled and spluttered as he showed Tobin through to an untidy parlour littered with books and army memorabilia.

'I was about to have a glass of beer. You care to join me?'

'That would be fine, Cap'n.'

Tobin settled in his chair, casting an eye over the crossed sabres pinned to the wall above the fireplace while Wallace poured out the two beers. He handed a metal pot across to Tobin.

'I've heard good words about you, Mr Tobin. You plannin' to stay in Bear Creek?'

Tobin shook his head. 'I have to get back east. I'm only stayin' around for—' he paused a moment before deciding to press on. 'I gotta tell you, Cap'n, Josh Devlin didn't die naturally. Seems he shot himself.'

Wallace took the pipe from his mouth. 'God rest his soul. Why would he do such a terrible thing?'

'I don't know, an' I'm beginnin' to wonder if he really did kill himself. That's not all. A no-good by the name of Masefield is plannin' to raid the bank. He's got a lotta men, an' he's well armed. Me an' Charlie Forbes need all the help we can get.'

'Masefield must know about the ranch money. Wilkins allus uses riders I can trust.' Wallace's pipe, back in his mouth, bubbled, and the old soldier blew out a long plume of smoke while he appeared to do some hard thinking. 'Sounds as if you'll need as many good men as you can lay your hands on. 'Tis a pity both Devlin men have now gone.'

'Both of 'em? You knew Josh's brother?'

'Sure I did. I recall old man Devlin as well.'

Tobin had a sudden thought. He reached in his vest pocket and pulled out the photograph found in Josh Devlin's vest. He handed it across to Wallace who took spectacles from his jacket.

'Is that Josh's brother?' Tobin asked.

Wallace peered at the photograph for a few seconds, then

shook his head. 'No, it ain't. George Devlin had big ears.' He looked up at Tobin. 'You know what happened to George.'

'I heard he died in Andersonville.'

'He did. One of thirteen thousand who died in that god-forsaken place. But it was the way he died that stuck in the craw of all right thinking men.' Wallace sucked noisily at his pipe. 'You ever hear of the Raiders?'

Tobin shook his head.

'They were Union soldiers who preyed on their fellow prisoners, stealin' from them, beatin' them if they tried to hold out. For extra food and drink they betrayed their fellows to that Swiss swine who ran the prison.'

'So was George Devlin shot by Johnny Reb?'

'He was, but not in the way I reckon you mean. George was tough, and planned to escape. But he only got as far as the deadline.'

Tobin jerked upright almost spilling some of his beer. 'Deadline! That was Josh's last word to Charlie Forbes.'

'It was a barrier outside the walls of the prison to stop escapes. Johnny Reb would shoot any Union soldier who they caught reachin' it. The Raiders sold George out.'

'What happened to the Raiders when the War was over?'

'The Army put 'em on trial and strung most of 'em up but one or two got away and disappeared.'

Tobin leaned back in his chair. Was it all coming together to explain Josh Devlin's death? He'd got important facts from Wallace and he'd have to do some hard thinking. But now he had to get back to the reasons for his visit.

'I got good reason to think that Masefield an' his men are gonna hit the bank. Me an' Charlie Forbes are ready to stand but we're gonna need help. How many Volunteers you got?'

Wallace sucked at his pipe. 'Twelve,' he said.

Jesus Christ! Tobin had expected at least twenty. At this

73

rate the town was likely to muster only a couple of dozen to stand against Masefield and his men. From what he'd seen in Ellisville he reckoned that Masefield could find thirty to ride with him. His dismay must have shown on his face prompting a grunt from Wallace.

'Two years or more ago I had coupla dozen Volunteers. Then we had the cholera 'round these parts. Took off a bunch o' fine men.'

'Numbers might not matter. In Finney's workshop we've found what looks like a Gatling gun.'

'Heaven save us!'

'If we can get it workin' Masefield's gonna be stopped. But I need help. You got a Volunteer able to fix it?'

'The Volunteers are good men an' they'll stand strong, but they were all men o' the line, good with a long gun.' Wallace paused, thinking. 'Bradden,' he said suddenly. 'Feller who bought the general store. He knows about guns. He's the man to ask.'

Tobin pushed open the door of the general store to see a tall, dark-haired man behind a counter weighing out iron nails for a homesteader in a bib overall and a straw hat over grey hair that fell to his shoulders.

While Tobin was waiting he wandered over to the gun racks pinned to the far wall over to his right. In front of the racks were display cases showing a variety of sidearms and a collection of knives. He turned as he heard the man behind the counter wishing his customer a good day.

'Mr Bradden?'

'That's me, Mr Tobin. You pleased the whole town when you brought back Janey Garner. What can I do for you? I gotta a coupla Navy Colts if you're seekin' to change.'

Tobin shook his head. 'No, I'll buy a knife but I need your

help with somethin' else. We've got a Gatling in Finney's old place. I wanna get it workin'.'

Bradden raised his eyebrows. 'You expectin' a war, Mr Tobin?'

'Lotsa no-goods gonna hit the town. Lead's gonna be flyin'.'

Bradden pursed his lips. 'I reckoned I'd finished with all that when the War ended.'

'You were in the army?'

'Sure I was. Followed General Stone tho' I didn't know much about soldierin'. Charlie Stone was a fine man an' those folks back east treated him real bad.' Bradden shook his head as if clearing his head of bad memories. 'I gotta tell you, I ain't got the tools if the Gatling's really broke. I can get 'em, but it'll take time.'

'Take a look, that's all I'm askin'.'

'OK. Mrs Bradden can look after the store if I'm away a while.'

Tobin stepped out along the boardwalk, his spurs jingling, keen to get back to the office and tell Forbes what he'd learned. Captain Wallace's mention of the deadline had changed everything. Had he been right in thinking that the soldier in the photograph was, indeed, Truman? Why would Josh Devlin carry a photograph of a man who he had almost certainly never seen in the flesh? Maybe Truman had been been a Raider at Andersonville. Could he have been responsible for the betrayal of George Devlin?

He pushed open the door to the sheriff's office and saw that two men were in the seats opposite the desk behind which Forbes sat. The sheriff looked to the door and the two men turned as Tobin stepped into the office.

'These two gentlemen just got off the stage,' Forbes explained. He turned to the older man of the pair. 'You'd best be tellin' my deputy what you've just told me,' Forbes said. 'Mr Tobin is sorta advisin' me on a few things.'

'I'm in Bear Creek from back east for a short while,' Tobin said. 'Me an' the sheriff work as a team.'

The older man looked at both Tobin and Forbes in turn, and nodded. 'This gentleman is Mr Daley,' he said waving a hand in the direction of his companion. 'I shall explain, but it's enough to say for now that Mr Daley saved my life a few weeks back.'

Daley's expression hadn't changed since Tobin had first walked into the office and taken his chair. Now he stared back at Tobin, unblinking, across the office. A gun for hire, Tobin decided, and made up his mind that he and Forbes would have to watch him. The older man reached into the deep pocket inside his coat and took out a leather document case which he placed on the desk.

'You will wish to examine those, Mr Tobin.'

Tobin looked down at the case. 'And why should I do that Mr. . . ?'

'My name, sir, is Henry Truman.'

Tobin's mouth twisted. 'There's a Henry Truman out at Clearwater.'

'No, sir. The real name of the blackguard at Clearwater is Max Hayter. He was responsible for the gang of ruffians who attacked me when I was leaving home to travel out west. They were intent on killing me when ordered to do so, but the Company hired men to find me. When the ruffians tried to shoot their way out, Mr Daley was forced to kill all five.'

Daley's eyebrows twitched slightly as if to indicate that killing five men was all in a day's work for him. Tobin wondered if he'd given the five men the chance to surrender, but Daley didn't look like a man who was strong on mercy.

He looked at the case placed on the desk by the man who

claimed to be Henry Truman. There was nothing to gain by inspecting the papers immediately. If the man's claim to be the real Truman was false he would have made sure the papers would pass a casual examination. He took the photograph of the soldier found on Josh Devlin from his vest pocket and passed it across.

'You know this man?'

Truman took spectacles from his pocket and peered at the photograph for a few seconds. 'This must have been made ten years ago, but that's Hayter. He was wearing those moustaches when he joined the Company. We got rid of him when we found he was stealing from our shipments.'

Tobin took back the photograph. 'If what you say is true, why would this Hayter pretend to be you? Even with the extra man he's hired he's not gonna rustle enough cattle to earn him more than a few dollars.'

Daley moved quickly to place his hand lightly on Truman's arm as if to discourage him from answering the question. The action surprised Tobin. He'd assumed that Daley was little more than a hired hand; maybe he was more than that in the New Amsterdam Company. Truman nodded in Daley's direction as if to acknowledge the warning.

'I can't answer that at the moment, Mr Tobin. A messenger will arrive with a letter. I shall know then what arrangements have been made.'

'Does it have anythin' to do with the money from the ranches?'

'Not as far as I know.' Truman stood up. 'What will you do now?'

Tobin remained seated. 'I'm gonna look at these papers. If they're OK, Max Hayter goes to jail. If they ain't, you and Daley here take his place. Meanwhile, you two gentlemen stay in town.'

CHAPTER EIGHT

'Watch those cottonwoods over to the right,' Tobin ordered. 'Last time I was here some no-good was skulking in the trees.'

Forbes nodded, his face grim, as he drew his long gun. 'We expectin' Truman, that's Hayter I mean, to put up a fight?'

'He ain't gonna give up easy, I reckon. But we got the advantage. Caleb Bolton tol' me Hayter goes out with him for a coupla hours every day. I reckon he'll not be expectin' us.'

Both men spurred on their mounts towards the Big House, and soon they'd reached a couple of large barns and brought the Clearwater ranch house in sight. Tobin reined in his palomino, looking ahead towards the ground surrounding the house. All appeared to be quiet. Ten yards from the house stood a buggy, the empty shafts resting against the ground. 'Hold it, Charlie. Let's make sure we both know what we're doin' here.'

Forbes drew alongside Tobin. 'Simple, ain't it? We go in, arrest Hayter, an' stick him in jail for the judge.'

'I hope it works out like that, Charlie. But we gotta be ready for the worst. I'd be damned easier if we knew where that no-good he'd hired was about.' He looked again at the ranch house. 'OK, we just ride up makin' it look as if we got more questions. Put your long gun down. Our Colts stay on our hips, an' we'll just look peaceful.'

'An' if it ain't?'

'We split up.' Tobin pointed to the small outhouse over to the left. 'You ride like hell and take cover, an' wait to hear from me.'

'What you plannin' to do?'

'I'm gonna make for that buggy.'

'If there's trouble, that's damn close to the house.'

'That's where you come in: I get to the buggy an' you keep 'em busy.'

'What happens if—?' Forbes broke off, reluctant to finish what he'd intended to say.

'You ride like hell back to town, round up the Volunteers an' hunt the sonovabitches down.' Tobin smiled grimly. 'But it ain't gonna happen.' He took up his rein. 'You ready to go?'

Forbes nodded, his mouth set, and touched his heels to the side of his mount. Both men kept their eyes on what lay ahead, their heads turning first to the left and then to the right as they approached the house.

Nothing stirred, save for the light breeze which brushed at the leaves of the small stand of trees over to the right of the house. The two men were about fifty yards from the Big House when the first shot rang out, kicking up dirt maybe three yards from Tobin's palomino.

'Go, Charlie!'

Tobin dug his spurs into the palomino, his head low down on the saddle, as he urged his horse towards the buggy. He felt the movement of air as a slug passed close to him and an instant later he heard the crack of the long gun. His heart racing, he reached the buggy, kicked his feet from the stirrups, and rolled from his saddle. He hit the ground hard, the impact forcing his breath from his body, and his Colt, still in its holster, digging painfully into his side.

His face in the dirt, he scrambled the last few feet to the buggy, snatching at his Colt. Jesus Christ! He was getting too old for this sort of play. He had a mental flash of the streets of Pittsburgh as he opened his mouth to suck in air. Maybe he'd gone past being beaten up and shot at. But there was nothing wrong with his reasoning. Hayter had someone in Bear Creek, that was certain. Someone who'd recognized the real Truman arriving in the stage and who'd ridden out to Clearwater.

There was a metallic screech as a slug ricocheted off the buggy wheel closest to the house. Risking a quick look, Tobin caught sight of a long gun protruding from a window on the upper floor of the ranch house. He twisted around to look towards the outhouse. There was no sign of Forbes's horse or of his own palomino. And where the hell was Forbes? As if to answer him, there were the sharp retorts of shots and the ratchet sound of a Winchester being reloaded. A window shattered, sending shards of glass flying down to the ground, a few of them peppering the buggy. It was time to make a move.

'You hear me, Charlie?' Tobin called.

'I hear you!'

'I'm gonna go for the house. You gotta keep their heads down.'

There was a pause so strung out that Tobin called out again.

'You un'erstan' what I'm tellin' you?'

'You do that, an' you're gonna get yourself killed,' Forbes called.

'You just keep their heads down when I call. You got that?'

'OK, I got it!'

Using his elbows, Tobin pushed himself up to a crouch hoping like hell that he was still protected by the large wheel and the side of the buggy. His Colt held in his right hand, his left hand flat against the ground ready to give a push forward, he took a deep breath.

'Now, Charlie!'

As he raced towards the steps of the house, in a half crouch, his head low, shots rang out from Forbes. Tobin heard the smack of slugs against the front of the house and again a window exploded scattering glass. From somewhere above came a strangled cry and the figure of a man pitched through the window and fell to the ground. Tobin barely glanced his way. Feeling his chest tightening, his lungs burned as he raced up the steps from the hardpack and threw himself through the open doorway into the hall of the house. He rolled behind a large chesterfield which stood to the left of the door. Then, pushing up on one knee, with his Colt held out before him, he surveyed the hall.

Nothing moved. He knew he was gambling his life on there being only two men in the house shooting at him and Forbes. One of those was now dead. Whoever was still alive knew he had to shoot his way out.

Then he heard the whimper. Had he not been still, his ears straining, he'd have missed it. There was silence for several moments. There! What sounded like a woman's muffled crying came from the end of the hall. Tobin realized it came from the room where he'd talked with Truman, or rather, Hayter, as he now knew him to be.

Using his left hand Tobin unbuckled his spurs – jingling metal as he crossed the boards could get him killed. He stood up slowly, his eyes firmly on the door which stood slightly ajar. Feeling his way across the polished wooden floor, taking each step slowly, he advanced to the door. Then, taking a deep breath, his Colt held high, he threw himself forward, crashing into the room.

'Just hold it there, Tobin!' Hayter shouted.

Hayter stood to the right of the desk, Janey before him on her knees, her head down, sobbing quietly. The barrel of Hayter's Colt was pressed against the side of her head.

Hayter leered across the room. 'You shoot me, she still dies.'

'Let her go, you sonovabitch. She's no part o' this.'

'And have you take me off to a hangin' judge? Put your Navy down, Tobin.'

'So you can shoot me?'

With his free hand Hayter hauled Janey to her feet. Still keeping behind her and holding on to one arm with a claw-like grip he pushed her forward across the room. Tobin's thoughts raced. Could he shoot Hayter without Janey being killed? Even if he were able to kill instantly, Hayter's reflex action could pull the trigger of his sidearm and kill the girl. Josh Devlin had asked him to get her back from Masefield. He'd done what Josh asked and he hadn't got the girl back to see her die a few days later. To hell with it! Let the Company catch up with Hayter.

'I'll make you a deal, Hayter. Let the girl go, an' you can hightail it outta here.'

'So that old bastard has told you who I am,' Hayter sneered.

'I'm givin' you a deal.'

Hayter's mouth twisted as if considering the offer. 'That Forbes feller ain't goin' to be chasing me?'

'The guns have spooked our horses. They're gonna take some catchin'.'

'OK, you gotta deal. Now drop that cannon and turn around.'

'How do I know you ain't gonna shoot me?'

'You'll have to trust me.'

Slowly Tobin uncocked his Navy and lowered his sidearm. His fingers uncurled and the Navy dropped to the floor. Had he just signed his death warrant?

'Now turn around.'

'You gonna shoot me in the back?'

'Turn around,' Hayter snarled.

Slowly Tobin turned. Fear clutched at his heart with such power that he thought he would vomit. Then his skull exploded, lightning chased across his mind, and he pitched forward into darkness.

CHAPTER NINE

'You can thank your ma for givin' you a hard skull, Mr Tobin, or you'd be spendin' the rest o' your days smokin' a pipe on your porch.' Doctor McKenzie twisted his mouth. 'Maybe you should have got yourself shot. I know a lot more about treatin' bullet wounds nowadays.' He stood back and admired the cloth around Tobin's head. 'I'm thinkin' of givin' up my other patients an' make a livin' outta you.'

'Thanks, Doc,' Tobin said ruefully. 'I'll stay outta trouble for a while.'

'You do that. Spend more time with Miss Summers.' McKenzie smiled broadly as he crossed to the credenza and poured water into the bowl from a tall jug. 'An' while I remember, tell Skippy that whiskey didn't fix his chest, nature did.'

'I'll tell him, Doc.'

There was a knock at the door as McKenzie was wiping his hands on a towel. The door opened at Tobin's call and Forbes stood in the doorway.

'Bradden's free now,' he said.

Ten minutes later Tobin and Forbes pushed through the door of the general store. They stood by the guncase while Bradden finished taking money from a young woman who picked up two small sacks from the counter. Tobin recognized Janey Garner as she turned away from the counter.

'Mother needed more sugar,' she explained. 'Mr Truman's got fancy tastes.'

'How is your ma?' Forbes asked.

'She's mournin' Mr Devlin,' she said. 'I wish now she'd married him when he asked her.' Her mouth turned down as she went past them and out of the store.

Bradden bid them good day. 'I've had a good look at the Gatling. How Finney got hold of it makes me wonder just what he was doin' 'round these parts. Anyways, I ain't able to help. It's broke an' I ain't gonna be able to fix it without more tools.'

'Then get 'em,' Forbes said. 'Nobody knows when we might need that pesky cannon.'

Bradden screwed up his eyes. 'Never agin, I'm hopin'. But I'll get word to Cheyenne.'

'Thanks, Mr Bradden. Let Mr Tobin know when they arrive.'

Both men wished Bradden a good day and left the store to cross Main Street, acknowledging the greetings of the townsfolk as they walked along the boardwalk. They passed the billiards saloon and then, from the barber's shop, a clean-shaven Captain Wallace appeared. Forbes and Tobin exchanged amused glances.

Wallace rubbed a hand over his chin. 'Darned beard was makin' me look an old man,' he said, a note of defiance in his voice.

'Sure makes you look younger, Cap'n,' Forbes said.

'You're gonna go far, Charlie Forbes,' Wallace said. The three men exchanged friendly grins. 'Anyways, to serious matters,' Wallace said, 'I got the Volunteers standin' by. You give the order an' they'll be ready an' armed. 'Bout time they earned that bounty the town's been payin' all these years.'

'That's fine, Cap'n,' Tobin said. 'I gotta question. You know anything about General Charles Stone?'

Wallace twitched his mouth. 'You sure come up with surprisin' questions, Mr Tobin.' He chewed his lip for several seconds. 'I got it now! Damned politicos jailed Stone after Ball's Bluff. Then they found it was the fault of the Oregon senator they'd made a colonel. Damn fool lost a heap o' good men. Thank God they brought Charlie Stone back.'

'Thanks, Cap'n. Good day, sir.'

'I reckon the cap'n is gettin' ready for a fight,' Tobin said soberly as they moved along the boardwalk heading for steps which would lead them down to Main Street. Tobin was aware that Forbes was shooting puzzled glances at him, obviously wondering about the last question he'd put to the captain. After a second's thought Tobin chose to say nothing. If he was wrong in what he was thinking there was no point in sending Forbes down the wrong trail. They were halfway across the street when Forbes stuck out a hand and pointed towards their office.

'Ain't that Miss Elizabeth's buggy?' He looked at Tobin. 'Are you an' her—?' He let the sentence slide away, a broad grin on his face.

'You might be sheriff, Charlie Forbes' Tobin said, 'but that don't stop me duckin' you in the horse trough.' He reached the steps up to the boardwalk a couple of paces ahead of Forbes and, a wide smile on his face, threw open the door.

'What the hell?' Tobin barked.

The man who was sitting by the stove, a tin mug in his hand, leaned back in his chair. He was dressed in trail clothes, his pants tucked in his boots, cavalry fashion, and on his hip he carried a .44 Army Colt with its eight-inch barrel. His leer showed that he reckoned he had nothing to fear.

'Take it easy, Tobin, I'm callin' the shots here.'

A bull-like roar came from Tobin who covered the space across the office in two strides. His hand shot out, grasping the man by his neck. He shifted his weight and heaved the man out of the chair. With a vicious kick to a point a couple of inches above the man's boot he sent him howling with pain to the boards. Shifting his feet as fast as a prizefighter Tobin lashed out with his boot at the man's stomach who again howled as he clutched at his middle. Once again Tobin shifted his feet, and raising one leg he made to stomp down on the man's face.

'Jesus Christ, Ben!' Forbes jumped forward and wrapped his arms around Tobin, heaving him away from the man who lay groaning, his hands in the air in an effort to ward off any further attack. 'Ben! You'll kill him, you don't stop!'

'They've laid a hand on Elizabeth, I'll kill the lot of 'em! An' their women!'

'Take it easy, Ben,' Forbes managed to get out, his breathing heavy, his arms still firmly wrapped around Tobin. 'We gotta talk with this no-good right now. It's gonna be no good he cain't talk.'

For several seconds the two men tussled around the man on the floor, Forbes flexing his muscles and using his strength to prevent Tobin from breaking free.

'Calm down, Ben! You ain't thinkin' straight.'

Tobin sucked in air. His arms became still as if he realized finally the good sense of Forbes's remarks. Forbes waited a few moments, and then, satisfied that Tobin had himself under control, released him and stood back, his stance showing he was ready to intervene if Tobin attacked again. But Tobin stood back. He walked across the office to stand looking through the window before turning back to see Forbes hoisting the groaning man on to a chair. Forbes made sure the man wouldn't topple to the floor and then walked over to pick up the tin mug. He half-filled it with coffee from the pot on the stove.

'Here,' Forbes said. 'Take some o' this, an' tell me what folks know you by.'

The man grunted. 'You don't need to know it.' He clutched at the mug and took a sip, his hand held against his chest. 'Goddamnit! I'm hurtin' real bad, an' I jest gotta deliver a message! I ain't even seen the woman.'

'Your name, stranger, or I'm gonna let the deputy at you agin.'

'OK! OK! The name's Collins. I'm tellin' you I just gotta give you a message.'

'I'm listenin',' Tobin said.

'You ain't gonna beat me agin?'

'Give me the message an' you ride outta here.'

Collins put a hand to his jaw as if checking to feel if it was broken before looking across the office, his eyes squinting at Tobin. 'Hayter says the woman will be fine if you do what he says.'

'An' what's that?'

'You gotta ride outta Bear Creek today an' don't come back. You do that, an' nobody will touch the woman an' she'll be let go.'

Tobin frowned. 'An' that's it? What does Masefield say?'

'Frank Masefield does what he's told. Hayter's the boss now.'

Tobin was aware that Forbes was staring hard at him. He turned back to the window overlooking the street and was silent for a few moments. Then, appearing to make his decision, he turned back.

'Tell Hayter he's gotta deal. I'll head for Cheyenne and go back east.' His mouth twisted. 'You tell him if he fails to keep his word, even if she lives, if it takes the rest of my life I'll hunt him down and kill him. You hear me? You give him that message like I've said it.'

'OK, I got that.'

The man rose to his feet, staggering a couple of paces before regaining his balance. Neither Tobin nor Forbes spoke as they watched him limp to the door and step out to the street. When the door closed Forbes started to speak, thought better of it, and lapsed again into silence. He walked to a chair, his head down. He appeared to be studying his hands as if across his palms was written how he was going to avoid getting himself killed.

'You think that sonovabitch believed my hogwash?' Tobin asked.

Forbes's head jerked up. 'You mean you ain't quittin'?'

'You're damned right, I ain't. I'm gonna wait a while an' then I'm gonna make a big show o' ridin' out.'

'You gonna sneak back?'

Tobin shook his head. 'I'm gonna ride to Ellisville. Miss Elizabeth needs me.' He smiled grimly. 'I sure ain't ridin' my palomino into Ellisville. Those no-goods would know me in minutes.' He almost smiled. 'I reckon the Wilsons are doin' fine outta me.'

A worried look had appeared on Forbes's face. 'You sure it makes sense goin' to Ellisville? You're gonna be one man agin a whole passel of them no-goods. I'm learnin' fast but I need you with me. I know I got the cap'n and his men but what happens if you get yourself killed?'

'Then you fight off Hayter and his bunch and make yourself the finest sheriff in the Territory.' Tobin punched Forbes lightly on his arm. 'But it ain't gonna happen, Charlie. I'm gonna be back as soon as I can with Miss Elizabeth.' He unfastened the star from his vest and placed it on Forbes's desk. 'I'm gonna be back for that, but right now I need to tell folks I'm quittin' Bear Creek.'

Five minutes later Tobin was doing another deal with the Wilsons at the livery. 'I'll leave my palomino for Miss Summers,' he said. 'You wanna sell me that roan back there you can name your price.'

'You bin good to me, Mr Tobin. Fifteen dollars the horse is yourn.'

They shook hands on the deal and the elder Wilson took the rig from the palomino and carried it over to the roan while he peppered Tobin with questions about big city life. As he tightened the final buckle he shook his head, sending the mane of his hair bobbing.

'I reckon city life's not for me, Mr Tobin, but I wish you Godspeed.'

Ten minutes later Tobin had paid his bill at the Majestic, and organized his boxes to be sent on by stage to Cheyenne. For a moment while talking with the hotel clerk he'd turned over in his mind the prospect of being back in Bear Creek and his boxes three days' ride away. Then inwardly he shrugged – either he'd be back to stop his boxes leaving with the stage or he'd be dead and it wouldn't matter. Finally, he walked into the general store and spoke with Bradden.

'When you get those tools for the Gatling let Charlie Forbes know.'

'Sure, Mr Tobin.' Bradden looked puzzled. 'Ain't you gonna be around then?'

'No, time I got back east. Bear Creek's a fine place but I must be about my business.'

Bradden nodded. 'Best of good fortune, Mr Tobin. Folks in town are grateful for what you've done.'

Tobin nodded. 'I'll be on my way.'

An hour later he was riding out of town.

*

Tobin rode for maybe a couple of hours before he started to look around for a stand of trees downwind from the trail. Ten minutes later he'd spotted a likely place on higher ground, and he turned the roan's head to cross the meadow and enter the shade of the trees. He slid easily from the saddle, and secured his mount, giving the horse enough freedom to nibble at the sparse grass beneath the trees.

Then he took up his position, sitting with his feet outstretched and his back against a tree. He was unsure how long he'd have to wait but he was guessing it would be worthwhile. He needed to find out who in Bear Creek was on Hayter's payroll. The no-good who'd brought back Elizabeth's buggy had ridden straight out of town with no chance of passing on a message. If his thinking was right, Hayter's hireling, anxious to be paid off once more, would be riding to carry the news of his own supposed departure.

Tobin put down his long gun and pulled out from beneath his shirt his small muslin bag of Bull Durham, keeping an eye on the trail while he rolled a smoke. He fished in the pocket of his vest for a match and a moment later he was breathing in the smoke, turning over in his mind how his life had changed these last few months: his enforced break from city life, the timely request from Josh Devlin, and his meeting with Elizabeth had all contributed to his being here, riding towards Ellisville.

The odds were against him, he knew that. But he had one big advantage: even if they doubted the message Collins delivered, Hayter and Masefield wouldn't expect him to risk his neck a second time. His stomach knotted when he thought of those no-goods holding Elizabeth captive. As fearful as she must be, he liked to think that she'd be waiting for him to come for her. Since that first day when he chased off the drunken cowboys he'd got the crazy idea that he'd known her all his life. They just hadn't met up before.

He crushed the remaining inch of his smoke into the damp earth around the base of the tree as the sound of a horse's hoofs reached him, the animal travelling at high speed. He picked up his long gun and scrambled to his feet as the rider came into view. Another hundred yards closer and Tobin could recognize who was losing no time in reaching Ellisville. He raised his long gun and for a second was tempted to shoot. He could kill Hayter's hireling as easy as shooting fish in a barrel, but maybe it was better to let things be for a while. If Hayter had any doubts about the truth of what he was told by Collins, those doubts would be removed when he received the same news from another source.

Tobin lowered his long gun and dropped to the grass once more as the sound of the rider began to fade. He'd give the rider maybe half an hour and then make for the trail leading to the north of Ellisville that Forbes had told him about. That way he'd avoid the risk of meeting Hayter's hireling returning to Bear Creek.

'Hold it there, stranger!'

The shout from behind a cluster of rocks came as a surprise. Tobin judged he was three miles from Ellisville and had seen no other rider since joining the trail from the north. He reined in the roan, and sat easily in the saddle waiting for someone to appear – there was nothing to gain by putting a scare into a nervous hunter or some innocent cowboy riding the trail. A moment later a tall, heavily built man stepped out from behind one of the rocks. He was carrying a long gun and on his vest was pinned a silver star.

'Keep your hands where I can see 'em, an' step down.'

Tobin didn't move. 'What the hell's goin' on? You lawmen aimin' guns at decent folks nowadays?'

'I ain't gonna tell you agin. Get down from your horse.'

Tobin shrugged. He stepped down and stood by his horse, not moving. 'Mr Masefield ain't gonna like this.'

The deputy hesitated at the mention of Masefield's name but still waggled the barrel of his long gun in Tobin's direction. 'Now you walk over here an' take it real slow so's I get a good look at you.' The deputy lowered his long gun an inch or two when Tobin stood a couple of yards away. 'You know Frank Masefield?'

'Sure do. Play poker with him. That's where I'm goin'.'

Doubt appeared on the deputy's face. He lowered his long gun further, sending Tobin's mind racing as he glanced down at the deputy's Winchester. Could he reach the long gun before it came up again and blew his head off? The deputy was staring at him as if reading his thoughts.

'I seen you before,' he said suddenly.

'That ain't surprisin',' Tobin said, his muscles tightening. 'I been visitin' with Frank mebbe a couple of months.'

The deputy shook his head. 'That ain't it.'

'The bathhouse mebbe? Took a bath in town coupla weeks back.'

The deputy shook his head. 'That ain't it,' he said again. He screwed up his mouth. 'Reckon it'll come back to me.' He stood back. 'OK, on your way.'

Tobin nodded, his muscles relaxing. He turned and headed back to his horse. There was no sense in getting himself killed before he'd even reached where Hayter was keeping Elizabeth, and he already had a good idea where she'd be.

'Jesus Christ! You're that Tobin sonovabitch!'

The metallic click of a sidearm being cocked behind him

sounded in the still air and Tobin pivoted on one heel. His Navy barked once and a fine red spray coloured the air above the deputy's head. Grey matter spilled to the dirt. The deputy was dead before his body hit the ground.

Tobin breathed in deeply, feeling his heart beating wild enough to break out of his chest. His gun hand was trembling as he slid his Navy into its holster. He'd have been dead meat if he hadn't been fast. He leaned over the back of his roan to pull his long gun from its scabbard then walked over to the deputy's body and bent to unpin the silver star.

'Goddamned back-shooter!' Tobin muttered. 'You ain't fit to wear this.'

He lifted his arm and sent the badge skimming into the bunch and buffalo grass beyond the rocks. He tossed his long gun on to the ground and picked up the deputy's weapon.

'Sure is a fine long gun,' he said aloud, feeling the balance of the Winchester '76.

Light was fading as Tobin left the trail and reached the hard-pack of Ellisville's Main Street. The noise of men's voices, the shrill laughter of the calico queens, and the sound of fiddle music, reached him as he passed the saloon. He kept his head bent, the brim of his hat pulled low on his brow. Only Hayter and Masefield and maybe a few of Masefield's men could recognize him but he was taking no chances.

He rode ten yards past the saloon, turned down an alley-way and rode to the rear of the saloon. He expected to be coming out of the saloon fast and it made sense to keep his horse close by. He dismounted, hitched his horse to a nearby rail, and pulled out the Winchester '76 from its scabbard. Checking the street was empty he crossed to the door out of which he'd brought Janey Garner and stood still for a few seconds. Then he pushed open the door and went up the back stairs to the corridor heading for Belle's room.

He opened the door to the passageway and the noise from the saloon hit him like the shock wave from cannon-fire. This close, the sounds mixed with each other to create a steady roar. Tobin realized that luck was with him; the timber men had been paid and were intent on spending their money before they returned to the forests. The noise they were making made a perfect cover. He kept his eyes on the doors until he reached Belle's room, turning the handle of the door to push his way in. Belle was seated at a table, dressed only in a shift playing cards against herself.

'You got the wrong room,' she said without looking up. 'Next door you want.'

'I got what I want,' said Tobin softly.

Belle's head snapped up. 'Jesus Christ, cowboy! Don't you ever stop tryin' to get yourself killed?'

'Just gimme the key, Belle. I get my woman then I'm gone.'

'What the hell you talkin' about?'

He changed the Winchester to his left hand and pulled his new knife from his boot top. 'It's you or her, Belle. I guess you just lost.'

Tobin took a step forward and then stopped suddenly as the barrel of a gun pressed hard into his spine.

'I'd say you're the loser, Tobin,' Masefield said, his voice only inches from Tobin's ear. 'Now drop all the iron you're holdin'.'

CHAPTER TEN

'Stop right there, Tobin,' Masefield ordered when they reached the door to The Hole. 'Belle! Unlock the door an' make sure you stay outta Tobin's reach.'

The two men stood still. Masefield's sidearm pushed hard against Tobin's spine as Belle stepped forward, key in hand, to unlock the solid oak door. The brass key turned easily in the lock as Masefield prodded Tobin forward.

'OK, get back to your room, Belle,' he said. 'I'll take care o' this.'

Neither man moved as Belle scurried past them. A moment or so later Tobin heard the slam of her door above the noise which reached up to him from the floor of the saloon. He breathed in deeply, tensing his muscles. Once he was in The Hole he knew he'd lose any chance of freeing Elizabeth. Although he could hear no sound from her, he guessed she was already in the room.

'The woman ain't gonna count for anythin' in all this,' Tobin said. 'You got what you wanted. Now let her go.'

A snicker came from Masefield. 'You ain't bein' fair to the lady's charms, Tobin. After Hayter gets back tomorrow an' me an' him shoot pieces off you, I'm promisin' myself a little party with your gal.' He prodded Tobin forward. 'Now get in there or I'll break my word to Hayter an' kill you now for what you did to my little brother.'

Tobin felt the sidearm taken from his back but before he could make a move Masefield's boot hammered against his spine and he was sent hurtling into the room to pitch forward on to his face as he heard the door being locked behind him.

He scrambled to his feet, aware in the dim light thrown from the small lamp in a nook of the wall, of a silent figure seated on the bunk at the end of the room. He peered into the shadows.

'Elizabeth?' Tobin asked.

'Oh, thank God!' The figure rose from the bunk, and took a pace towards the centre of the room; Tobin recognized the ash-white face of Elizabeth. He held out his arms, and she rushed forward, throwing herself against him so hard he had to take a short backward step to keep his balance.

'I knew you'd come, Ben! You'll get us out of this terrible place. I know you will!'

Her arms around his neck, Tobin made soothing noises as he stroked her hair, not trusting himself to speak. Damn Masefield to hell! How was he going to bust out of this place with twenty or more men against him, and Hayter, when he finally got back here, determined to kill him? And if Hayter didn't finish him Masefield surely would, determined as he was to avenge the death of his brother.

Tobin had been in tight corners before and had always managed to fight his way out, but this was different. He had no gun and he had Elizabeth to protect. They'd be hunted down like animals. He gently unfastened Elizabeth's hands from around his neck.

'Let me take a look at the walls. Mebbe there's a spot we can break through. Masefield's not comin' back until the mornin'. We got plenty o' time to plan our escape,' he added with more confidence than he felt.

'Is there anything I can do?'

'No, you just sit on the bunk an' rest.'

He led her back to the bunk, and attempted an encouraging smile as she sat down. Then he moved to the walls and began an inch by inch search. It didn't take long for him to realize he was wasting his time. The walls were of solid oak from floor to ceiling. He'd need a six-pound axe to break through them. He looked above him but the ceiling was out of reach even if he stood on the bunk. He guessed the saloon had once belonged to the timber company and the room had maybe been a store for valuable items or even for the takings from the surrounding homesteads. Nevertheless, he took the best part of two hours checking there were no flaws in the walls which might lead to their making an escape. Finally he got to the point where he'd started.

'Is there a chance?' Elizabeth asked.

He shook his head. 'We have to face it,' he said, moving to sit beside Elizabeth on the bunk. 'There's no way out.'

Her head went down. 'Oh, my God! What will happen to us?'

He put an arm around her shoulders. 'You'll be OK. I'm the one they want outta the way. Hayter's a no-good but he's not an animal. When they've raided the bank at Bear Creek they'll let you go. I'm sure of it.'

'But Masefield—' Her voice faltered, and she turned her head away.

Tobin breathed in heavily through his nose. 'He'll not kill you, I'm sure of it. He'd gain nothing, an' I'm sure he'll let you go.'

She lowered her head to rest against his shoulder, 'Ben,' she said slowly. 'It's what he said to me before you came. I've

98

never—' Again her voice faltered, and she made a tiny whimpering noise.

'Hush,' Tobin said softly. 'We'll face them tomorrow. Try to get some sleep.' Gently he extricated himself from her grasp and stood up. 'I'll take the floor. I'll be right beside you, an' who knows what will happen tomorrow.'

His hand resting gently on her shoulder he eased her down on the bunk, grasping her hand for a final second as she laid her head on the rough material of the pillow. As she closed her eyes, he stood looking down at her for a few seconds before he stepped away from the bunk to lower himself to the floor, pulling off his hat to serve as a rough pillow. His fingers touched the bandage put on by McKenzie and was relieved to find it dry. Then his mouth twitched – what the hell did it matter if the bandage was dry or not?

He had closed his eyes for only a few minutes, sleep a long way distant, his mind racing, when the silence was broken by Elizabeth, jerking him out of his thoughts of what was likely to happen the following morning.

'Ben, are you awake?'

He waited a few seconds before replying. 'Yes,' he said.

'Ben, what Masefield said—'

'Hush, Elizabeth, don't dwell on it.'

There was silence for a few seconds before Elizabeth spoke again.

'Ben, I want you here with me,' she whispered. 'I'm not going to think about tomorrow. I only know I want you with me tonight.'

Tobin closed his eyes, uncertain at first how to respond. He pushed himself up to a sitting position, his head only a couple of feet from Elizabeth who had turned on the bunk to face him. He saw her smile, her face pink in the gloom, her eyes wide and clear as she looked at him steadily. Then she reached out her hand to grasp his shoulder and his arms enfolded her.

'Ben Tobin! Ben! Can you hear me?'

Tobin's eyes snapped open. Again the insistent whisper reached him. He looked down at the still sleeping figure of Elizabeth, cradled in his arms. Had he imagined the whisper? No! There it was again!

'Ben Tobin? Can you hear me?'

Tobin pulled away his arm and, bootless, moved quickly to the door, dropping to one knee to place his ear to the keyhole. Now the whispered call was clear. 'Ben Tobin! It's Charlie Forbes! For Chris'sakes wake up!'

Tobin put his mouth to the keyhole. 'I'm here, Charlie. We're both here.'

'Then take cover. I'm gonna blow the door!'

Tobin sprang up, raced across the room, pushed his feet into his boots and with one scoop of his arms lifted the still sleeping Elizabeth. He dropped to one knee and thrust her below the bunk as her eyes opened, confused and frightened at what was going on. Not bothering to explain, he pressed his body against her beneath the bunk. His fingers went to her face and he forced her mouth open, while she made choking sounds trying to get out words.

He bared his teeth an instant before the door behind him was hurtled across the room in an explosion which blasted at his ears. Sharp stabbing pains scoured his back as if a hundred needles had penetrated his shirt, undervest, and skin. Dust and smoke filled the room as he scrambled from beneath the bunk, heaving Elizabeth with him. He released her for a moment, to scramble to his feet then grabbed her arm and hauled her to her feet, both of them coughing violently as they were unable to avoid inhaling the dust from the explosion.

Holding Elizabeth's arm, he ran her across the room towards the doorway where Forbes stood, a Colt in each hand. Forbes thrust one into Tobin's hand as he and Elizabeth reached the doorway. Forbes's face, covered in dust, showed a grim smile.

'The whole town's gonna be up an' about. Let's get the hell outta here!'

Forbes spun around as a figure appeared at the top of the stairs and he loosed off a shot, not bothering to take real aim. The figure dropped out of sight, footsteps loud on the stairs.

'The door!' Forbes shouted.

The three of them pushed through the door and went down the back stairs, Forbes running ahead, Tobin holding on to Elizabeth's arm, pulling her after him, ignoring her attempts to suck in air and clear the choking dust that had entered her body. Forbes flung open the street door, throwing up his hand to point across the street.

'Make for the wagon!'

They raced across the street to the wagon which stood in the light of the early dawn. The wagon driver hooded and cloaked, clutched in a raised hand a whip, ready to set the two horses moving. Tobin raced to the rear of the wagon and half lifted, half pushed Elizabeth through the break in the canvas, hearing her strangled scream as she thumped on the hard boards of the wagon's interior. Snatching a quick glance along the street he saw a movement at the side of a building. For an instant a shadow shifted along the street and Tobin fired two quick shots, not expecting to hit anything but determined to keep anyone from following them.

He raced to the front of the wagon, boosting himself on to the hard wooden seat along Forbes and the driver. The whip cracked above the horses' heads as they moved forward in a walk. After five yards they broke into a trot, and then, urged on by another crack of the whip, they broke into a gallop.

Tobin drew a deep breath. He turned to pull the canvas aside so he could see into the wagon. 'Elizabeth? You OK?'

He saw she was on her knees facing him, holding on to the side of the wagon as it bounced and shook. Her face was pale but her mouth was set firmly. She didn't speak but she nodded vigorously and while he remained studying her, her mouth moved and she managed a smile.

Reassured, Tobin turned back to Forbes who sat alongside him, a long-gun across his knees. 'Guess I owe you, Charlie Forbes,' he said.

Forbes turned to face him, and grinned. 'Couldn't handle all this on my own. Had to bring help.' He nodded in the direction of the driver who put up a surprisingly slim arm to push back the hood.

'Charlie needed me to show where they'd keep you,' Janey Garner said.

CHAPTER ELEVEN

Caleb Bolton was on the steps of Clearwater's Big House when Tobin and Forbes arrived shortly before noon. The same boy who'd been standing alongside him on a previous visit ran down to take their horses when Bolton waved a hand in their direction.

'Fine lookin' boy,' said Tobin as their horses were led away.

'A Clearwater range boss in mebbe twenty years, I reckon,' Bolton said. 'His ma should've lived to see him.' A shadow passed across his face for an instant. 'What can I do for you lawmen?'

Tobin reached the top of the steps, Forbes alongside him. 'We're gonna look over part of the house.'

Bolton reacted as if stung. 'Now hold on! What the hell you mean by that?'

'It's what Mr Tobin's just said. We're gonna search part of the Big House,' Forbes said. 'You gonna be ornery, an' we're gonna be seein' Mr Truman.'

'Mr Truman an' Daley are out looking at beef we got on the high ground. They ain't gonna be back afore nightfall.'

'Yeah, we heard that. You want we come back tomorrow? This way we reckon it makes things easier for you,' Tobin said.

Bolton looked at him hard. 'I saved your goddamned carcass once. Mebbe I was a mite hasty. I ain't sure how Mr Truman's gonna feel about you pokin' through his house.'

Tobin shrugged. 'It ain't as if we're gonna go all over the house. We just want to have a look around where Beth Garner and Janey do most o' their work.'

'What the hell for?'

'We ain't sure,' Forbes said. 'But we'll be quick about it. You get Janey an' her ma to some other part o' the house, an' only you'll know what we've been about.'

Bolton appeared to turn this over in his mind for a few seconds. Then he nodded. 'OK, I'll do it.' He stopped suddenly as if something had occurred to him. 'This ain't to do with the message Mr Truman's waitin' for?'

Tobin shook his head. 'This is somethin' else.'

Bolton held his gaze for a second or two before turning on his heel.

'Wait here,' he called over his shoulder. 'I'll be back.'

'He's bein' mighty careful,' Forbes said slowly after Bolton had pushed through the wide double doors and disappeared into the house.

'S'pose that makes him a good range boss,' Tobin said. 'I reckon he's straight up but if he's lyin' I reckon he oughtta go back east and join a playhouse.'

Forbes chuckled. 'Cain't see Bolton in fancy clothes an' paint on his face.'

The two men were exchanging amused looks when the big door to the house opened and Bolton reappeared. 'OK, I cleared the way. You wanna follow me?'

A few minutes later, after they'd walked through the house along a passageway with walls showing dark oil paintings and stone carvings standing in small alcoves they reached the working kitchen of the house. A long table dominated the centre of the room around which half a dozen chairs stood. On the left hand side of the room stood grey painted cupboards. Tobin guessed they provided food storage for the occupants of the house. On the end wall, an open fire showed flames flickering up from the wooden logs large enough to keep the fire burning for most of the day.

Beneath a table next to a stone sink stood pots and pans. By the sink, fixed below a window, a black iron pump with a tail-like curved handle stood ready to provide water. Rows of glass jars showing dark-coloured fruit stood in an open cupboard, opposite the sink. Bolton pointed to the small archway at the end of the room.

'Through there you got all the plates an' stuff Beth uses for the house. You wanna look through that?'

'No, this is fine. You gonna stick around or can we make a start?'

'I'll be back in an hour. You'll be through lookin' then.' Bolton made it a statement of fact and not a question. Without waiting for an answer he turned on his heel and left Tobin and Forbes alone. Both men watched him, waiting until he'd closed the door before they bent to release their spurs, placing them on the table in the centre of the room.

'You take that end of the room,' Tobin said, pointing in the direction of the alcove. 'I'll start this end. If we find anythin' it's gonna be on the floor, I reckon. We're damned lucky it's stone. I reckon Bolton wouldn't take kindly to us ripping up boards.'

Tobin turned to walk to the end of the room and dropped to his knees so he could reach below the bottom shelves of the cupboards as he worked down the length of the room. Forbes did the same. Slowly they searched along the wall against which stood the sink and above it, the window. When they were only a few inches apart, Forbes broke the silence.

'I hope we ain't wastin' our time.'

'I'm not sure, Charlie,' Tobin said. 'Mebbe we are. I reckon we got time to try the other side afore Bolton comes back.'

The two men got to their feet and crossed the room to drop to their knees once more, scrabbling with fingers beneath the cupboards and shelves. Tobin was a quarter of the way along the room when his fingers closed over what he'd suspected he might find.

'Got it, Charlie!'

As Forbes clambered to his feet and crossed the room Tobin stood up and held out what he'd found. In the light thrown into the room through the window the coin-shaped silver gleamed in the palm of his hand.

'Josh Devlin's medal. Mebbe he thought Beth Garner had already returned, and came here to see her. There must have been some sort of confrontation between Josh and Hayter, an' I'm guessin' Josh was shot here and moved to his office as he was dying. Josh meant to leave this here or mebbe it spilled from his pocket.' Tobin stared hard at Forbes. 'I reckon the Raider who sold out Josh's brother was Hayter and Josh recognized him from the picture he carried. They shoulda strung up Hayter in Andersonville, now I got two reasons to kill the sonovabitch.'

Tobin and Forbes hadn't been back in their office more than five or ten minutes when the street door opened and in stepped Henry Truman and Daley. They looked as if they'd been riding hard, dust clinging to their trail clothes. Truman had lines of stress around his eyes.

'I guess you're lookin' for coffee,' Tobin said.

He crossed to the tin mugs and poured hot coffee from the pot that had been bubbling away since first light. 'Caleb

Bolton tol' me you were out lookin' at your beef,' he said, as he handed over the mugs.

'A small fiction on my part, Mr Tobin,' Truman said. 'Mr Daley and I had a meeting with a rider carrying a message for me.'

'You don't trust Bolton?'

'I've no reason not to, but I prefer to be careful.'

'I guess as you're here the message is gonna concern me an' Sheriff Forbes.'

'Yes, that it does.'

Tobin's mouth twisted. 'Mr Truman, I'm tryin' to show my good manners but you're makin' it a mite difficult for me. You gonna tell me what's goin' on?'

Truman's eyes flickered towards Daley who shrugged and drew heavily on the cheroot he'd lit when he'd first taken his coffee. Truman clicked his teeth appearing to consider his words.

'There's a wagon due to arrive here in Bear Creek tomorrow from Deadwood carrying a hundred thousand dollars worth of gold.'

Tobin exchanged glances with Forbes who pursed his lips in a silent whistle. 'An' does Hayter know about this?'

'Yes, I'm sure he does.'

'Hayter's smarter than I thought. I was guessin' he was after the ranch money in the bank.'

'There's no more than five thousand dollars been brought in,' Forbes said. 'It's a heap o' change and if Hayter got his hands on it he'd have pulled off the biggest bank raid in the county. But the wagon's gotta be what he's after.'

Tobin shifted to address Daley. 'Hayter's got over twenty men armed with Winchester '76s. He musta been plannin' this for months. You better get back on your horse an' stop that wagon from comin' any closer to Bear Creek.'

Daley shook his head. 'I cain't do that.'

Truman cut in. 'The Company has a big deal going down in Cheyenne. That gold has to be there within ten days or the deal collapses. The plan is to hold the gold here for a couple of nights, and then more men will come to Bear Creek to escort the wagon to Cheyenne.'

Forbes smacked his hand down on his knee in anger. 'Now hold on! This is plumb crazy! You're puttin' the whole of Bear Creek at risk. Anyways, why the hell you doin' business with gold? For crissakes, you're goin' back twenty years!'

'Now Sheriff—'

'When I took on the job I hadn't planned for a god-damned battle along Main Street!' Forbes cut in. 'This is a decent town with decent folks. We're mighty short of Volunteers but the men we got will stand strong. But you gotta remember they have women and children an' work to do. An' we ain't fancyin' on seein' bodies along Main Street!'

There was silence in the office for several moments. Tobin breathed in deeply and replaced his pen carefully in the inkwell on the side of his desk. For several moments he stared out of the window, his mouth set in a hard line. Then he swung back to face Truman.

'How many men with the wagon?' Tobin asked.

'Eight,' Daley said before Truman could answer. 'Two driving the wagon, four riders, an' two sharpshooters inside the wagon.'

'Does Hayter know how many men are with the gold?'

'No. I didn't know myself until today.'

Forbes stood up. 'I'm tellin' you all, now. We gotta aim to keep these scallywags outta Bear Creek.' He moved to the wall where a map of the district was pinned. His forefinger traced along a line leading from the north to the town. 'The wagon's gotta come this way. Hayter sure ain't gonna try an' take the wagon on the open ground. There's only one place where he could mount an ambush and that's around Johnson's Creek. We're gonna be outnumbered but we got ex-soldiers an' they know how to handle a shootout. Hayter's men are a bunch o' no-goods. I'm guessin' they'll scatter.'

'That's smart thinkin', Sheriff,' Daley said. 'What you reckon, Mr Tobin?'

'If it keeps gunfighting out of the town then I go along,' Tobin said.

'Mr Daley will join you, Mr Tobin,' Truman said. 'I only regret that my days for such shenanigans are over.' He got to his feet, preparing to leave. 'I'll pay every man who sees the wagon into town a reward of fifty dollars.'

'I'm gonna take a room at the Majestic for a coupla nights,' Daley said. 'You'll find me there when you need me.'

'You got a notion when the wagon should reach the Creek?'

'Mebbe an hour after noon tomorrow.'

'OK. Be ready to move outta here coupla hours after dawn.'

The posse, led by Tobin, reached the ground around Johnson's Creek before noon. As the men reined in to form a semicircle, Tobin turned his palomino's head so he could face them.

'OK, you all know a bunch o' no-goods are gonna try an' take the wagon an' we're here to stop 'em. Cap'n Wallace has tol' me you all got women and children so I'm gonna say it once. Any man decides to ride back to town ain't gonna be thought worse of.' He paused. 'But if you stay, you stay to the end.'

Several of the men exchanged glances but none of them spoke. Tobin looked around at the riders. 'We got eight men with the wagon; two of 'em are ex-Army sharpshooters.'

'Hope they're Johnny Rebs,' called out one of the men. 'They were better than ourn.'

There was a burst of laughter, and several cheers. Tobin, grinning, held up a hand. 'OK, I'm plannin' we'll be back in town by sundown. Hayter an' Masefield know if they let the wagon reach town then they know they're up agin the bank.'

Tobin hoped what he'd said was near the mark. He and Forbes had talked about Hayter and Masefield waiting for the wagon to reach town. But Hayter, at least, had been a soldier, and must know that he'd need at least double the number of men defending the bank, and furthermore he'd be up against the new safe the Company had installed for Wilkins.

'Cap'n, take your men to the creek,' Tobin ordered. 'We'll take the high ground. If Hayter an' his men show up I reckon we'll see 'em comin' but we ain't gonna take chances. Make sure you put one o' your men so we can see him.'

'OK, Mr Tobin.' Wallace shifted in his saddle to pull a wad of red cloth from his saddle-bag. 'He'll show this we get sight o' those scallywags.'

'That's good thinkin', Cap'n.'

Tobin dug into his own saddlebag, pulling out an old blue trail shirt. He tossed it across to Wallace. 'Have your man show that if the wagon passes you an' Hayter hasn't showed. Then we'll know you're ridin' to join us. I ain't takin' chances.'

Wallace, Daley, and the men of their posse began to move away when a thought occurred to Tobin. 'Mr Daley! I'm thinkin' o' the men on the wagon. They know who you are?'

'Don't concern yourself, Mr Tobin. They know me. I ain't fancyin' bein' shot to pieces by some sharpshooter.' With a grim smile, Daley put a finger to the brim of his hat in mock salute and turned the head of his horse to move up alongside

Wallace, both men ahead of the bunch of Volunteers.

Tobin watched them for a while. Wallace was no longer a young man but the men would follow him. He wasn't sure he trusted Daley. He'd be a good man in a fight and his job was to protect the gold for Truman and the Company. Unless, that is, he'd been paid more to do something different. Anyways, if Daley had sold out there was nothing he could do about it until Daley showed his cards. Tobin turned the head of his palomino and looked up the slope of the high ground.

'We'll take a position among those cottonwoods,' he called to the remaining half dozen Volunteers. 'Fine if you wanna smoke a pipe, but keep any fires on the small side. Hayter an' his no-goods are gonna come from the north. We'll have one man posted lookin' thataways, an' we'll have one lookin' east. Another man will be posted to watch for Cap'n Wallace's man. Sentry duty to last an hour. The Sergeant'll make out a routine. We could be waitin' a long time.'

He touched the sides of his mount with his spurs and led the riders up the hill, Forbes a few yards behind him.

Four hours had passed since Tobin and his posse had reached the shelter of the cottonwoods. The Volunteer sergeant had organized lookouts and the men, having checked their weapons, had settled down. Some had stretched out on the grass, some were seated on the ground with their backs supported by the trunks of the cottonwoods.

The men, all ex-soldiers, knew how to spend their long hours of waiting for what might be only a few minutes of action: one was trimming his beard with a battered pair of scissors and the help of a small cracked mirror; two were playing cards with a greasy pack that should have been thrown away a long time ago; another was peering at a small black book which might have been a Bible; two men, their backs against trees, were dozing, their heads dropped almost to their chests.

Tobin had shifted his position until he could see both to the north and towards where he could look across the open meadows in the direction of Ellisville. He looked up at the watery sun. Another couple of hours the light would begin to fade and he knew that Hayter would have to make his move soon.

He looked around at the group of men and for a moment wondered what the hell he was doing in Wyoming Territory sitting on a log which was beginning to give him an aching butt. When Josh Devlin called on him for help he hadn't hesitated. Sure, it was lucky he could take time out of Pittsburgh but he'd have come anyway. He'd owed that much and more to his old partner. Maybe he should have left Bear Creek after bringing Janey Garner home. Devlin had never fully explained why he felt it necessary to call on him but it wasn't hard to guess the reason.

He had to admit that only his pride, after he'd been bushwhacked in the livery, had kept him in the town. He smiled to himself. Well, that and the prospect of seeing Elizabeth Summers as many times as he could. He looked up as a shadow moved.

'Mr Tobin! The wagon's on the way.' Macklin, the sergeant of the Volunteers, had crossed the open space between the trees to speak in a low urgent voice. 'Sentry's seen the signal from Cap'n Wallace.'

Tobin pushed himself off the log. 'Get the men mounted an' we'll ride to meet up with him. Have a man at the rear to keep a lookout.'

A few minutes later Tobin led his group down the slope from the high ground. As they reached the hardpack of the trail, the wagon, surrounded by riders, was heading towards him. As he turned his palomino's head in their direction he saw Daley break away from the group and race towards him. Daley held his hand high.

'Everythin's fine,' he shouted as he grew closer. 'No sign of Hayter.'

Tobin stood up in his stirrups and turned to face the men behind him.

'Sergeant Macklin! Take two men and ride point. Rest o' you ride behind the wagon.'

As Daley grew closer the wagon began to slow, and a rider on a big grey broke from the group surrounding the wagon and caught up with Daley as he reached Tobin.

'This here feller's Tom Marcle,' Daley said. 'He's ramrod-din' this outfit.' He turned to Marcle. 'This is Ben Tobin I been tellin' you about.'

Marcle nodded. 'Glad you could meet us, Mr Tobin. Sounds as if I coulda run into trouble.'

'We ain't at the bank yet, Mr Marcle. Best we get there as fast as we can.'

Without waiting for an answer he glanced towards the wagon, now halted, to check that all the men were in their positions, and then turned to head for Bear Creek.

'What the hell's that smoke?' shouted the tall Swede driving the wagon.

Tobin had been riding at the rear of the wagon as they approached the town and he spurred his mount forward to get a better look at what the wagon driver had seen. The Swede was pointing his long-handled whip in the direction of Bear Creek. Above the outline of the town's buildings plumes of black smoke stained the pale light of the evening sky.

'Slow the wagon!' Tobin shouted. What the hell was going

on? He swung around in his saddle calling out to one of the Volunteers.

'Jackson! Your mount as fast as it looks?'

'Sure is, Mr Tobin.'

'Charlie! You an' Jackson ride into town an' find out what's goin' on. Then get back an' tell us. An' Charlie, you keep in mind that Hayter could be in town.'

Without hesitating the two men dug spurs into the sides of their mounts and within moments were lost from sight around a bend of the trail.

'We're gonna halt here until they're back,' Tobin called up to the Swede. 'No sense in ridin' into somethin' we don't know.'

The Swede acknowledged the order, touching his whip handle to the brim of his hat before easing back on the reins, bringing the four horses down to a walk and finally to a halt.

Marcle brought his horse alongside Tobin. 'What you reckon?'

Tobin grunted. 'I reckon Hayter's made damn fools of us.'

'You reckon he's waitin' there?'

Tobin shook his head. 'Cain't be too careful. Warn your sharpshooters we could be ridin' into trouble.'

'I'll do that,' Marcle said.

Tobin sat relaxed in his saddle, aware that the Volunteers behind him were beginning to voice their concerns to Captain Wallace. He didn't blame them. Sat out here waiting for news when it was possible that a bunch of no-goods was beating up the town wasn't an easy hand to play.

Marcle came back. 'OK. They've been told.'

As Marcle moved away Tobin saw Captain Wallace break away from the group of Volunteers, his raised hand acknowledging something said by one of them. Wallace walked his horse across to Tobin.

'The men are gettin' restless,' the captain said. 'They don't like what they're seein' with all that smoke. They wanna make sure their homes are safe.'

'Tell 'em to wait until Charlie Forbes gets back. It'll only take a few minutes more. Then we'll know what's goin' on. It ain't likely their homes have been touched, an' they got fifty dollars comin' their way.'

'That smoke could mean anythin'.'

'Yeah, it—'

Tobin broke off as from the bend in the trail Jackson came riding hard towards them. Jackson's roan kicked up the dirt of the trail as he hauled back on the horse's head bringing the animal to a skittering halt.

'Charlie Forbes stayed in town, Mr Tobin. Hayter an' his no-goods hit the bank but they been an' gone!'

'An' the smoke?'

'Some o' the stores on fire. Them sonovabitches blew Mr Wilkins's safe right out. Front o' the bank an' what's left of a coupla stores are in the middle o' Main Street. Them no-goods musta used enough powder to blow up Cheyenne!'

CHAPTER TWELVE

'Christ,' said Tobin aloud, his hands on his hips, surveying the wreckage.

Groups of a dozen or more townsfolk stood on the hard-pack of Main Street, huddled together as if for self-protection. Several men milled around without apparent aim, their faces pale with shock. Women were openly weeping and small groups of men were talking in low voices between themselves. Tobin was aware that many of them were looking at him with angry expressions across their faces.

The front of the bank had been reduced to a pile of broken stones and splintered wood. The interiors of the stores either side, strewn with rubble, were exposed to view. In the bank, among scattered piles of papers, a gap in the mahogany counter showed where the heavy iron safe had been blown off the rear wall of Wilkins's office. Tobin realized it must have first torn through the thin board which separated the office from the counter area. Then the safe had smashed through the counter and been flung twenty feet across the boardwalk and into the middle of Main Street. Now the empty safe, its door wide open, lay in the dirt surrounded by the debris of the three buildings.

The wife of the townsman who owned the dry goods store

next to the bank let out a sob of despair as she and two companions desperately tried to gather up the rolls of cloth that lay around. The big broad-shouldered German who owned the store on the other side of the bank was dragging what remained of his barber's chair.

'Ben! What the hell we gonna do?' Forbes's face was taut with shock.

Tobin didn't reply directly. Instead he addressed the wagonmaster. 'Mr Marcle. Have the Swede drive the wagon into the yard behind the sheriff's office. Charlie'll show you where it is. Keep your men with the wagon.'

He turned to Wallace. 'Cap'n, ask the Chinaman to get the men some grub an' coffee. I'll see the mayor, an' the town'll pay.'

'Sure thing, Mr Tobin.'

'You wanna talk with Mr Truman?' Daley, standing alongside Wallace, looked around at the groups of townsfolk. 'He ain't here so I guess he's at the hotel. We'll find him in that fancy private parlour they got there.'

'You're damn right I wanna talk with Truman,' Tobin said.

Tobin and Daley walked their mounts across to the rail outside the Majestic and then went up the steps to enter the hotel. Three men were leaning against the clerk's desk. Their conversation ceased abruptly as they saw Tobin crossing the hallway in the direction of the private parlour. Truman stood up from his high-backed chair as Tobin and Daley entered the room.

'I thought it better to stay here,' Truman said. 'Is the gold safe?'

'That all you got to say, Mr Truman?' Tobin said harshly. 'Hayter and Masefield shoot up the town, wipe out the bank, ruin God-fearin' townsfolk, an' all you can think about is your damned gold?'

His boots sounded on the polished boards as he stepped smartly across the room to the window, looking across Main Street towards the sheriff's office. Two men, rifles in hand, stood at the end of the alleyway. Marcle must have posted a couple of men while Forbes was seeing the wagon safely into the yard. As Tobin watched, the Chinaman and his son crossed Main Street both carrying large pans. Steam rose from around the edges of the tin covers. Tobin turned back to the room.

'Yeah, you got your gold, Mr Truman. How long you're gonna hang on to it is another matter.'

Truman who had sat down again, raised his eyebrows, seemingly unfazed by the sharpness of Tobin's voice. 'Marcle and his men will take it out to Clearwater until the Pinkertons arrive from Cheyenne.'

'An' how long will that be?'

'Three days, maybe four.'

Tobin looked across at Daley who pulled up his mouth but said nothing.

'Mr Truman,' Tobin said, his voice more even. 'After what Hayter's done to Bear Creek he'll be expectin' you to take the gold to Clearwater. You do that an' Hayter's gonna find out damned quick. Don't fool yourself He's gonna come after the gold. You'd be gettin' all the folks at Clearwater killed.'

'Mr Tobin's thinkin' right,' Daley said. 'A cattle ranch is no place for a gunfight.'

'I'm telling you now we're not going to try and shift the gold to Cheyenne without the Pinkertons,' Truman said.

'No, that would be damned crazy,' Tobin agreed. 'I'm suggestin' we keep the gold in town an' make sure Hayter knows. He'll come into town an' we'll be waitin' for him.'

Truman frowned. 'How can you make sure he'll know?'

'I gotta way to do it.'

Truman looked at him for a few seconds waiting for more but when Tobin remained silent he put another question to him. 'You're sure Hayter and Masefield will try for the gold? The money from the ranches is probably more than they've ever taken before. Why shouldn't they hightail it out of the Territory?'

'Hayter's thinkin' big. I reckon he's been plannin' this ever since he was workin' for your Company back east. He ain't gonna be satisfied with a few thousand from the ranches.'

Before Truman could reply there was a knock at the door and Daley stepped across the room to open it. The hotel clerk stood in the doorway, an apologetic expression on his face.

'I'm sorry to disturb you gentlemen. But the mayor would like to see Mr Tobin. Mayor Parker is in the other parlour.'

'Tell him I'll be along,' Tobin said.

'I'll do that,' the clerk said, and closed the door.

Truman looked irritated by the interruption. 'So where do we keep the gold, Mr Tobin? Mr Wilkins's safe is no longer possible.'

Tobin smiled grimly. 'We'll stick it in the jailhouse. When Hayter arrives we can fall back there if needs be but I'm gonna study on how to stop those no-goods afore they get too close to any gold. Now I gotta see the mayor. If there's nothin' else I'll see you gentlemen later.'

He nodded briefly and then left the room, closing the door of the private parlour door behind him. He paused for a moment before crossing the hotel hall to the other parlour. For all the assurances he'd given to Truman he was guessing that in ten minutes' time the councilmen would have taken his badge and he'd be preparing to leave town. He took a deep breath, reached the door of the parlour which was ajar and pushed straight through. On the other side of the room five chairs in a line were occupied by the mayor flanked by four other men whom Tobin, as far as he aware, hadn't set eyes on before.

'Mayor Parker, I hear you got things to say to me.'

'Take a seat, Mr Tobin.'

Parker waited until Tobin sat, glancing to both left and right before clearing his throat. 'What's happened to the town today has been a disaster, Mr Tobin.'

'Yeah, I hate to see a good town like this hit by those no-goods.'

'You left the town without defences, Mr Tobin. I know Charlie Forbes is sheriff but we all know you're making the decisions.'

Tobin's mouth twisted, and for a moment he was silent. Then he spoke.

'I agree. I gotta confess Hayter outwitted me,' he said. 'I was sure he was gonna go for the wagon we just brought in.'

Parker frowned. 'And why would he do that?'

'Cos the wagon's packed with gold from Deadwood.'

Tobin saw the jaws of the five men drop simultaneously. On the far right, the councilman sporting a floral vest beneath his Prince Albert let out a startled shout. Anxious looks were shot at Parker.

Tobin touched the badge on his shirt. 'You wanna take this from me? I guess that's what this meetin's all about. You reckon I fouled up an' I ain't hidin' that from you. You got right on your side.'

'Now hold on, Mr Tobin,' Parker said hastily. 'Nobody's talkin' about any firin'. Anyways, not now. We didn't know about the gold. You keep that badge on your shirt.' Parker again exchanged glances with his councilmen before turning back to Tobin. The four men remained silent and Parker turned back to Tobin.

'Why the tarnation is a wagon o' gold in Bear Creek?'

'The Company folks are shippin' it for a deal they got down in Cheyenne. Their Pinkerton men'll be here in two or three days to see it safe.'

Parker let out a sigh of relief. 'Then we got a straight answer. The gold goes to the Clearwater ranch.'

'You gonna stand back when all the folks at Clearwater get gunned down by Hayter an' his no-goods?'

The councilman to the right of Parker stroked his beard. 'Mr Tobin's right, Henry. Put the gold out at the ranch an' Hayter's gonna go for it. Lotsa folks gonna get killed.'

'William, you telling me we keep the gold here?' Parker barked. 'So how many townsfolk you wanna see killed? Hayter an' his men will wreck the town.'

'That's been done,' Tobin said. 'But there's a way back. We can clear the townsfolk to a safe place. You stop Hayter an' Bear Creek's gonna be standin' real high with the New Amsterdam Company. They'll pay for the bank an' I reckon they'll pay for the stores. Down in Cheyenne you men are gonna be well thought of. Important folks will see you as havin' stood up for law an' order.'

For a few moments there was silence in the room. Tobin studied the men's faces as they turned over in their minds the decision they were about to take. One, his hands clasped across his floral vest was looking openly doubtful. Maybe, thought Tobin wryly, he had the least political ambitions. Parker, from what Charlie Forbes had told him, had his eye on bigger things than being mayor of Bear Creek. The prospect of being well thought of by the power brokers in Cheyenne may just have won his support.

'OK,' Parker said. 'But from what I hear Hayter's got

plenty of men.'

'I tell you all somethin' an' it stays in this room,' Tobin said. He waited until all five had nodded their agreement. 'We got the men who brought in the wagon to stand with us. Two of 'em are ex-army sharpshooters. That's gonna help stop Hayter an' his no-goods.'

'Lawdee me! I seen one o' them sharpshooters durin' the War,' exclaimed the councilman called William. 'He made our life real hell.'

Tobin got to his feet. 'If we've finished here I'll be on my way. I gotta see Mr Bradden over at the store.'

'He's not at the store,' Parker said. 'He's a fine council-man and he shoulda been here today but Doc McKenzie has him in his back room. Bradden's a lucky feller. Doc took a slug out of him, an' says he'll make it. Bradden deserves somethin' from the town. Bravest thing I ever did see.'

Tobin frowned. 'What happened?'

'Those no-goods had been in town a while, a group of 'em outside the bank. They musta been waiting for the powder to be set. Folks had fled from Main Street, scared outta their wits. Then Miss Peabody, the schoolmarm, comes walking down the street as if she was goin' to church. I guess she had no notion of what was goin' on. This no-good goes after her and scoops her up across his saddle. She's hollerin', the rest o' those no-goods are shoutin' an' I don't like to think what was goin' to happen. Then Bradden comes rushin' out of his store. He ain't carryin' a gun but he throws himself at the horse's head, an' in all the shoutin' and cussin' an' screamin' Miss Peabody gets away and runs for her life down by the livery stable.'

'An' what happened to Bradden?'

'No-good swears he's gonna kill him. Shoots once an' Bradden goes down. The no-good's gonna shoot again when

122

the bank an' the stores go up like crazy. All the no-goods charge into the bank an' Bradden is left lyin' in the dirt. The doc an' two other men run out an' pick up Bradden an' carry him into the store.'

Tobin's mouth twisted. That sure changed what he'd been thinking only moments before. But he kept his face expressionless and bid Parker and the councilmen a polite good day.

'Howdy, Doc.'

McKenzie, dark shadows beneath his eyes, and lines of strain showing on his face, looked up from behind his desk. He pushed away the book he was writing in and placed his pen on the brass inkstand which stood at the edge of his desk.

'We have trouble on our hands, Mr Tobin.'

'You heard about the gold?'

'Charlie Forbes has just left me. He was warning me that I'm going to be busy the next few days.'

'I'm tryin' to ride 'round that, Doc. I hear you have Bradden in your back room. Can he talk?'

'Yes, he's awake. Hurtin' darned bad but he'll be OK.'

'Can you strap him up so he can ride?'

McKenzie raised his bushy eyebrows. 'He'd hurt like hell. Why you asking?'

Tobin ignored the question. 'But he could ride if he had to? For a few hours?' He saw McKenzie hesitate. 'It's important, Doc.'

'I could give him laudanum to carry, I s'pose,' McKenzie said slowly. 'But you gotta give me a darned good reason.'

'OK. Can I see him now?'

'I'll show you through.'

'I wanna do this on my own, Doc. No offence.'

123

McKenzie stared at him for a few seconds. Then he nodded. 'Very well.' He pointed to a door in the corner of the room. 'He's through there.'

'Thanks, Doc.'

Tobin crossed to the door and entered the room where Bradden was propped up in bed, his back against the frame of an iron bedstead. His eyes were closed. Above the rough blanket he was bare save for the large bandage which swathed his shoulder. At the top of his arm, the stain of blood showed through the grey-white of the bandage.

Tobin crossed the room to the bed and picked up the cane chair from in front of the stucco wall. He spun the chair so he could sit with his arms resting on the back of the chair. Bradden opened his eyes. For a moment they were cloudy but then they cleared.

'Howdy Mr Tobin,' he said.

'Heard you did somethin' today lotsa men woulda been proud of,' Tobin said.

'Miss Peabody's a good gal. That no-good woulda—' Bradden's voice trailed away.

'I got some questions for you, Mr Bradden. You OK to answer?'

Bradden gave a brief nod. 'Doc's done a great job. I'm a lucky feller. What questions you got?'

'First off, Mr Bradden, you can tell me how much Hayter's been payin' you to tell him what was goin' on in town.'

There was silence in the room for a few seconds. 'What the hell you talkin' about?' Bradden muttered.

'After I tol' you I was leavin' town you rode as damned fast as you could to Ellisville. You reckoned you had news for Hayter.'

'Listen—'

'I saw you, Bradden. So don't waste my time by lyin'.'

'I thought—'

'I don't give a damn what you thought. You're gonna get off that bed an' ride to Ellisville. You're gonna hurt real bad but you'll do what I say. Now listen up! This is what you're gonna tell Hayter.' Slowly, repeating himself when necessary, he instructed Bradden on what he was to tell Hayter.

Tobin crossed Main Street from the doctor's house, cut through the sheriff's office and went through to the back yard. In the centre stood the wagon, still with the horses between the shafts, chomping away at the feed in their morrals. Marcle and his men sat on the ground around the wagon, their rifles alongside them. There was no sign of Captain Wallace and his Volunteers.

Forbes came across to Tobin. 'The cap'n let his men go to see their families. They'll be back to keep watch after dusk. That'll give Mr Marcle an' his men time to get some shut-eye.'

'Good work, Charlie. Have Marcle an' his men unload the gold and stow it in the cells. He can fix who sleeps out here or inside. We're gonna have to guard this place for a while. Truman's sent to Cheyenne but we'll be here for mebbe two or three days afore the Pinkertons arrive.'

'I hear the mayor wanted to talk with you.'

Tobin grinned. 'He was gonna fire me, I reckon. Then I tol' him about the gold.' He looked around the yard, his smile fading. 'I gotta take a walk for a while. You get every-thin' here movin'. I'll be back an' then we got some plannin' to do.'

'That's fine by me, Ben.'

Tobin knocked on the door of Elizabeth's clapboard. He waited several minutes, growing increasingly impatient, and

125

was about to knock more loudly when the door opened.

'Hey, Millie—'

He stopped suddenly. Elizabeth stood in the doorway. She was pale, and her red-rimmed eyes showed that she had been crying. Instinctively, Tobin stepped forward, his hands going to her shoulders.

'Are you OK? What's happened? Where's Millie?'

Elizabeth said something but her voice was weak and he failed to catch her few words which drifted away. He leaned forward and gently lifted her chin until he was looking into her eyes.

'What happened?'

'Someone came looking for me when Hayter and his men rode into town.'

Tobin felt as if an icy hand gripped around his heart. He wouldn't shoot the son of a bitch who'd laid a hand on Elizabeth. That would be too quick.

'I wasn't here,' Elizabeth said. 'I'd spent the whole day with the Ruskin family out at the homestead. By the time I'd finished with Emma it was growing dark and Mrs Ruskin insisted I stay the night. I only came back an hour ago.'

Tobin breathed in deeply. 'But where's Millie?'

'Oh, Ben, she was beaten badly when she tried to stop that blackguard coming into the house.'

'Do you know who it was?'

Elizabeth shook her head. 'Millie can't speak. Her mouth—' Her voice trailed away, and she looked down.

'Can I see her?'

'Of course. She's in her room at the back of the house.'

Elizabeth stood back to allow Tobin to enter. He slipped off his gunbelt and hung it over the wooden peg before following Elizabeth through to house.

'Have you sent for the doctor?'

126

'Yes. But he's been delayed. He's busy with Mr Bradden for something.'

'I know about that. He'll be here soon.'

Elizabeth pushed open the door to the small room where Millie lay beneath sheets on a narrow bed, her head on a rough cotton pillow. Elizabeth moved to the window and opened curtains so Tobin could see Millie better.

Silently, Tobin swore. Millie lay on her back, the light falling on her face which was covered with black bruises. Her flesh had swollen, showing her eyes as mere slits as Millie moved her head an inch, trying to see who had come into the room.

'Mr Tobin's here to see you, Millie,' Elizabeth said softly.

From between cut lips Millie attempted to speak until Tobin put a finger to his lips. 'Hush, Millie. Doc McKenzie will be here soon.' Tobin looked up at Elizabeth for a moment, before looking down at Millie again. 'Now I want you to do something for me. I want to ask you a couple of questions.' He leaned forward and gently took the girl's hand.

'Can you squeeze my hand?' He smiled as he felt pressure on his own hand.

'Good girl. Now I want you to squeeze once to say "no", and twice to say "yes". Can you do that?'

'Good girl,' Tobin said again, as he twice felt the pressure from Millie's fingers.

'Now listen, Millie. Back in Pittsburgh a fine lady's gonna want to have a really smart maid. Miss Elizabeth will have to decide, 'cos she was gonna send you to a big house in Cheyenne. But would you like to go to Pittsburgh if Miss Elizabeth agrees?'

His smile broadened as Millie's fingers pressed twice against his, and then twice again before his smile faded. 'Now

127

I'm gonna ask you about the man who came here and hurt you. Is that OK?'

Satisfied that he'd received a positive reply, he pressed on.

'Was it the man who was in town last year? Was it the man who took away Janey Garner?'

He felt the two squeezes on his fingers, and looked up at Elizabeth.

'Masefield,' he said. 'Thank God you weren't here.' He looked down at the girl again. 'You've been very brave, Millie. Now don't you forget what I said about Pittsburgh. Doc McKenzie will be here soon an' you'll be on your feet in no time.'

When Tobin and Elizabeth had quit the room and were in the hall leading to the street door, Elizabeth put a hand on Tobin's arm. 'Will you really take Millie back east with you?'

'Only if you agree,' he said.

'When do you plan to leave?'

'As soon as I can,' Tobin said, buckling on his gunbelt. 'But first I got work to do and a debt to settle for Josh Devlin.'

CHAPTER THIRTEEN

Doctor McKenzie stood up from behind his desk, an angry expression on his face. 'Just what the hell are you up to, Tobin? I open my door this morning to find Mr Bradden on the ground. He was covered in blood and couldn't say a word. I shouldn't have listened to you and your crazy notions. You could have killed that man.'

'Where is he now?'

'He's in my back room. And that's where he's staying.'

'I gotta talk to him.'

'You are not going in there! I am the doctor in this town, and I'm telling you that he's too sick.'

Tobin breathed in deeply. 'Doc, you got every right to take a stand but you gotta believe me. I promise you I'll explain tomorrow.' That's if I'm still alive, he added to himself. And if he was dead an explanation wouldn't be worth spit on a rock to anyone. 'I need no more than a coupla minutes. You have my word.'

McKenzie's expression said clearly that he was torn between his conscience as a medical man, and believing Tobin. He grunted loudly and sat down suddenly as if his legs had given away.

'Two minutes. Not a second longer. And don't get him all fired up.'

Tobin breathed in deeply. 'I just want your word that you'll not tell anyone about Bradden ridin' last night.'

McKenzie looked hard at him for a few seconds, then nodded briefly.

'OK. I just hope to hell you know what you're doing.'

'Thanks, Doc.'

Tobin pushed through the door and saw Bradden was in the same bed. Instead of being propped up against the bedframe he was flat on his back, the rough blanket pulled up to his chin. From the doorway, Tobin could hear his laboured breathing – he didn't have to be a doctor to know that Bradden might not make it. He shrugged away his doubts about what he was doing and crossed to the bedside. He bent low so his mouth was only a few inches from the storekeeper's ear.

'Bradden,' he said. 'It's Tobin.'

Bradden's eyes flickered, and pink spittle ran from the corner of his mouth as he appeared to try to speak. He gave a wet cough and more pink spittle trickled down his chin. Tobin bent closer to the man's ear so that his face almost brushed Bradden's head.

'Did you get to Hayter?'

Bradden lifted his head an inch. 'Yes,' he said. His head fell back on the pillow, and he again closed his eyes.

'And Marcle? Did you tell him about Marcle leavin' town at dawn tomorrow?'

'Yes, yes I did.' Tobin could barely hear Bradden's words. 'Hayter's comin' tomorrow.'

A grim smile appeared on Tobin's face. 'You did just fine, Bradden.'

'Hayter made us took damned fools last time, Mr Tobin.'

Captain Wallace stood at the front of the crowd of men

who filled the office, a few paces behind the chair in which Truman was sitting. 'How can you be so sure he'll not come in today? Come to that,' Wallace went on, 'mebbe we're gettin' our pants on fire for nothin'. Hayter's got the money from the ranches. Why's he gonna risk his neck for more?'

'He's gonna go for the gold,' Tobin said. 'I'm sure of it. I reckon he's been plannin' this ever since he worked for the Company back east.' He looked to the corner of the office. 'You wanna say anythin', Mr Truman?'

Truman, who sat alongside Daley shifted around in his chair to address the men. 'I think Mr Tobin is on the right track. In two days the Pinkertons will be here to see the gold to Cheyenne. So you men need to hold out until then. The Company will be generous to men who make a stand. Meanwhile I've paid Mr Marcle and his men to stay until the Pinkertons get here.'

'But you're gonna earn that money. You'll still be out-numbered,' Daley pointed out. 'Jest like you woulda been at Johnson's Creek. Hayter's gonna hire anyone he can. He gets his hands on that gold an' he can pay off every no-good who rides with him, an' he'll still have plenty of money for hisself an' Masefield.'

'Hayter's had a spy in town tellin' him what's been goin' on hereabouts,' Tobin said. 'I'm not givin' you his name but he's told Hayter that Mr Marcle an' his men are leavin' tomorrow at dawn. We've got time to get ready.'

There were noisy protests from the Volunteers. One of them shouted out: 'We gotta spy in town, we want the name of the sonovabitch!'

Tobin held up his hand in the face of more angry shouts. 'You're gonna have to trust Charlie an' me on this. I reckon Hayter'll wait until late mornin' or noon before he makes his move. Mr Daley's right. Hayter'll reckon he needs all the

131

men he can get. Takin' on a town, ready an' armed, is gonna take a lotta men and he'll aim to get his hands on as much gold as he can.'

Tobin looked around at the men, satisfied from their expressions that he'd carried them with him. He just hoped to hell he'd got the situation right. All the Volunteers were married men with children. If Hayter came in with thirty or forty men, there was the risk of a bloodbath; women in the town could be widows and their children fatherless.

'Somethin' else. When I've done here I'm gonna have a talk with Doc McKenzie. He'll be fixin' things if anyone stops lead an' needs lookin' at.

'What happens if we don't make it?' a fair-haired Volunteer asked. 'I gotta family to think on.'

'I've talked with Mayor Parker. We'll take money from the town's taxes,' Wallace said. 'No family's gonna go short.'

'OK,' Tobin said loudly. 'I'm gonna talk with Cap'n Wallace now. You men go about your business an' you'll be hearin' from him.' He turned to Marcle. 'I'm gonna need you here. Then you can tell your men later.'

Marcle nodded. 'Sure.'

Tobin rested his butt against the edge of his desk while most of the men filed out of the office. Forbes crossed to the stove and poured coffee for the men who remained. He offered a mug to Truman who waved it away.

'Mr Daley will look after the Company's interests in this matter,' Truman said. 'I'll just say that the Company will honour the promise we have with the town if the gold is safely delivered to the Pinkertons.' He picked up his hat. 'I wish you all good fortune.'

Nobody spoke until he had left the office. Then to Tobin's surprise Wallace let out a whoop of glee.

'You know what this means, Charlie Forbes?'

'One per cent,' said Forbes with a broad smile. He turned to Tobin. 'Last year the Company agreed to pay one percent of any money we safely shipped through Bear Creek. We've lost the ranch money but this makes up for it in damned spades.' He slapped his hand against his thigh. 'Mayor Parker's gonna be fair dancin' when he hears this.'

'You ain't there yet,' Daley said. 'Hayter's no fool, an' he's got Masefield with him an' some real no-goods.' He turned to Tobin. 'I sure hope you gotta plan for all this. I don't fancy cashin' in my chips in Wyoming Territory.'

Tobin didn't reply directly. He crossed to the stove and picked up a blackened piece of wood. He stepped to the wall and was about to start explaining his plan when the door opened and Caleb Bolton stepped in.

'I guess I'm too late,' he said. 'I just seen the Volunteers leavin'.'

'What can we do for you?' Forbes asked.

'I hear there's gonna be trouble. I got five good men with me. All of 'em seen time with the cavalry. We're gonna stand with you.'

'Men could get killed,' Tobin said.

Bolton nodded. 'They know that, they ain't fools.'

Tobin turned to the wall and raised the blackened piece of wood again. With half a dozen sweeps on the stucco he drew a rough map of Main Street and the half a dozen alleyways between the stretches of boardwalk fronting the stores.

'Cap'n, there are plenty o' wagons in the town,' Tobin said, using the blackened wood as a pointer on the wall. 'Afore dusk I want every alleyway blocked with a wagon. You reckon you can fix that?'

'I can fix it, no trouble,' Wallace said. 'But that ain't gonna keep 'em out.'

'I ain't aimin' to keep 'em out.' Tobin's mouth twitched.

133

'I'm aimin' to keep 'em in.' As the men in front of him exchanged puzzled glances, he turned to Forbes. 'The Wilson brothers at the livery, will they stand?'

'They're damned good with horseflesh, but they ain't likely to be much use with guns. Tho' they ain't lackin' courage. When the stage horses spooked last year they was right in among 'em.'

'OK. We're gonna need their help, so go talk with 'em, Charlie, after we're done here.' He made two further sweeps across his rough map, one at each end of Main Street. 'Josh Devlin once told me about a sheriff named Lannigan whose town was attacked by an armed gang. If the Wilson brothers reckon they can do what I need we'll put Hayter an' his men into the dirt.' In a few brief sentences he explained what he intended to do, and where he would place the Volunteers. When he'd finished he looked at each man.

'I ain't sayin' the plan's perfect but it's the best I can come up with. Anybody wanna say somethin'?'

'That's a mighty smart plan, Mr Tobin,' Wallace said. 'You'll have 'em trapped.'

'Hold on, Tobin,' Daley cut in. 'S'posin' Hayter does come in with thirty or forty men? You think they're gonna just sit there on Main Street? They're gonna be shootin' at anythin' that moves.'

There was silence in the office for a few moments until Tobin answered.

'You're right. An' what we gotta avoid is a bloodbath. We lose any o' the Volunteers an' that's gonna be a tragedy for some family. But we get a heap o' no-goods dead on Main Street an' Bear Creek's never gonna be the same agin.'

'It makes sense to clear Main Street o' the townsfolk,' Bolton said. 'But why you got Mr Marcle's wagon standin' outside the drygoods store?'

'We gotta take a chance but I reckon it'll work,' Tobin said.

The men listened attentively as Tobin explained what he had planned.

Tobin found McKenzie again seated behind his desk when he pushed open the door of his room. The doctor looked up with a frown and put down his pen.

'This time I mean it, Mr Tobin. You're not going into the back room.'

Tobin shook his head. 'That's not why I'm here. I'm gonna need your help tomorrow.'

McKenzie sighed and leaned back against the high back of his chair. 'Let me guess, Mr Tobin. There's going to be shooting, men are going to get hurt, and you'll be asking me to patch them up so they can go out again and get themselves killed.'

'The men here come through tomorrow and Bear Creek's gonna be quiet again an' a much richer town. Folks were talkin' about buildin' a real hospital and payin' some of the womenfolk as proper nurses.'

McKenzie's mouth twitched into a brief smile. 'I don't know what you do back east, Mr Tobin, but you sure know how to sing a sweet song. So what is it you want this time?'

'I want a place any man wounded can get to afore it's too late for 'em. You could use the saloon.'

McKenzie shook his head. 'Skippy helped me a lot when we had the cholera here but I'm not sure I'd trust him too close to whiskey. I'll need a few girls to help me with hot water and stuff. They'll not be easy in the saloon. I'll speak with Henry Parker. The mayor owns the Majestic and he's a good friend of mine. The big parlour just inside the hotel would be the place.'

135

'Thanks Doc. I'm obliged to you.'

'I'm not doing it for you. I'm doing it for Bear Creek.' McKenzie frowned. 'And that gets me thinking, Mr Tobin. You owe Bear Creek nothing. Yet from what I hear you're going to risk your life tomorrow. You're protecting the gold of a far off distant beef company and the reputation of a small western town. I wonder about your motives.'

'Would Josh Devlin have done the same as I'm tryin'?'

'Yes, of course.'

'Then you've got your answer.'

He saluted the doctor with a raised hand, and stepped out on to the boardwalk. A smile replaced the grim look on his face.

'Howdy, Elizabeth.'

Tobin raised a finger to his hat as he paused beside the buggy in which Elizabeth Summers was sitting, reins in one hand, a small leather pouch on the seat beside her. As she turned to face him he was taken aback by her expression. Beneath her eyes were dark shadows and the soft skin below her bonnet was lined with worry. Her blue eyes were blurred with the hint of tears.

'Oh, Ben, I've just heard there's going to be trouble tomorrow.'

'Don't you worry. We're well prepared. When Hayter and Masefield see what they're up against they'll choose to ride on.'

Elizabeth brushed at her eyes with a gloved hand. 'Ben Tobin, don't you dare treat me like a child. Those wretches are not only after the gold, they intend to kill you. The whole town knows the gold is in the jailhouse, and that means Hayter knows. They'll not ride on.'

Tobin looked to his left and right, checking that other townsfolk were out of earshot. 'The gold's not in the jailhouse. We shifted it last night.'

If he thought this news would calm Elizabeth he was wrong. Her free hand shot out and grasped his arm. 'Then you're going to risk your life for nothing! You'll be killed. We'll never again—' She broke off suddenly, her whole face flooding pink. 'I mean. . . .' her voice trailed away. She lowered her head to stare hard at the reins in her hand.

Tobin reached out a hand to gently lift her chin, leaving his hand on the side of her cheek. 'Now listen to me, Elizabeth. I'm not plannin' to get myself killed tomorrow. A lot of important people are waiting for me to get back to Pittsburgh, an' I don't intend to let them down. An' I ain't plannin' to let Josh down, neither. He'd have gone up agin Masefield and Hayter on his own if he'd had to. I'm luckier. I got plenty of good men to back me up. Nighttime tomorrow, Masefield an' Hayter are gonna be in jail or dead. Now you go back home an' stay there.'

Elizabeth managed a weak smile, and her fingers touched his hand briefly as he stepped away. 'I have to see Doctor McKenzie before I go home.'

Tobin frowned. 'You ain't sick?'

'No. He pays a few girls to do the fetching and carrying when he has to. I organized them for him when we had the cholera here.'

'When did he ask you?'

'Last evening. He came to see me.'

Tobin couldn't resist a smile. McKenzie, it seemed, was a step ahead of him.

A couple of hours before noon the sheriff's office was crowded. Mayor Parker and Doctor McKenzie stood against the door leading to the jail. Either side of the stove stood Forbes and Skippy. The two brothers from the livery, Harry and William Wilson, were by the window a few feet from Marcle. In the centre of the office, Captain Wallace was surrounded by his Volunteers. Tobin was about to speak when the door opened and Caleb Bolton stepped in.

'Guess I got here just in time,' he said. 'I can tell my cowboys what's goin' on.'

'Glad to have you with us, Mr Bolton.'

Tobin looked around at the men in front of him. Parker was almost grey with worry. How much was that worry down to the possible killing of townsfolk and how much was it down to Parker's own ambitions? If the gold was taken and men were killed, his political hopes for an eventual role down in Cheyenne would be dead meat. The taut faces of the Volunteers showed their stress. They were expected to turn out for public holidays and mount guards for important visitors to Bear Creek, they weren't expected to take on a marauding bunch of killers. Sure, they'd all had experience in the army but that was a long time ago when they hadn't wives and families to look after. Only Captain Wallace, a gleam in his eye, looked as if he was spoiling for a fight.

'Hayter knows we'll try an' hold out for the Pinkertons to arrive, but he has no notion of how strong we are,' Tobin said. 'I've seen for myself how many men he can call on.'

He picked up the blackened piece of wood and scratched a couple of crosses on the rough map he'd drawn previously, before turning to Wallace. 'I want two men with long guns, high up, on the Majestic. Charlie will be at the hotel door from the boardwalk. He'll give covering fire if any man needs the help of Doc McKenzie.' He looked across at Bolton. 'I'm gonna put you an' your cowboys with scatterguns in what's left of the bank. You easy with that?'

Bolton nodded. 'That's fine.'

'OK, I'll be in here at the windows with a coupla

138

Volunteers. The rest of the Volunteers will be split between the windows of the stores along Main Street and the wagons in the alleyways.' Tobin looked around at the group of men. 'Hayter's gonna come at us hard. We're gonna be outnumbered if he brings all the no-goods he can round-up.' A grim smile showed on his face for a moment. 'But we gotta coupla cards up our sleeve. First, you gotta know what the Wilson brothers are gonna be doin'.'

The elder Wilson from the livery stood forward and told the men exactly what he and Tobin had worked out the previous evening. There were cheers when he'd finished.

'Now it's Mr Marcle's turn to say his piece,' Tobin said.

'Two hours before noon the Main Street's gonna be clear,' Marcle said. 'Mr Tobin will have had all the townsfolk cleared well away. Hayter an' his men will see only the wagon we used to bring in the gold.'

'Hayter's never gonna think the gold's still in the wagon,' objected one of the Volunteers.

'He ain't meant to. It's what we got in the wagon that's gonna make him think he's made the biggest mistake of his life.'

CHAPTER FOURTEEN

Tobin stood outside his office looking up and down Main Street. Nothing stirred. The morning's breeze had died away almost as if nature herself were hiding from what would strike at the town in the next few hours. Tobin guessed the street hadn't been this quiet since cholera had struck. Now Bear Creek would have to hold out against a man-made disease: the greed for gold and the efforts of ruthless men ready to kill for a share of the yellow metal.

Standing alongside Tobin, Forbes pointed towards Marcle's wagon standing on the hardpack opposite the dry goods store. 'Hayter's gonna be damned wary o' that wagon.'

Caleb Bolton, alongside Forbes, snickered. 'Hayter's gonna be worryin' about more than the wagon if the day goes our way. The Wilson brothers from the livery do their job an' ourn is gonna be a damned sight easier.'

Tobin looked up at the sky, checking the position of the sun, estimating that Hayter would arrive in the next hour or so. The town's defenders would have maybe half an hour to ready themselves. One of the townsmen, now an old man, but once a Union Army tracker, had volunteered to ride out and keep watch.

'My hand ain't so steady no more,' he'd told Tobin. 'But I still gotta good pair of eyes.'

Tobin smiled grimly, recalling Wallace's words to his men as he ordered them to their positions. 'You wanna get a good look at what's going on just stick your head up. But don't come whining to me when some no-good shoots it off.'

'You reckon Marcle an' his men will stand?' Forbes said.

'He'll be fine, I reckon,' Tobin said. 'An' he's got Daley in the wagon with him.' He turned to Forbes. 'Charlie, take a walk around. Make sure none o' the townsfolk are still lingerin'. We got enough to study on. I'll take a walk over to Doc McKenzie. See if he's fixed up.'

Forbes's lip curved a fraction. 'Sure, an' give Miss Elizabeth my best wishes.'

An hour later silence had fallen over Bear Creek. The townsfolk had done as ordered, quitting their clapboards and stores in Main Street. Most of them had moved out to friends in the homesteads, the remainder had loaded buggies and driven into the stands of trees which were to the south of the town a few miles away.

Three old men who shared a tumbledown clapboard at the end of town had refused to move, telling Forbes they'd had good lives. If Hayter and his no-goods came shooting at them the town would have to bury them because none of the three had any money. After ten minutes of argument Forbes had given in and left them to take their chances.

Now Tobin, with a couple of Volunteers alongside him scanned the street, watching the men taking up their positions he'd detailed. From the half a dozen two-storey buildings he reckoned the men would command the length of the street with the weight of the fire levelled at the area around the jailhouse.

He looked across the street, and raised his hand, acknowledging the wave from Forbes who stood in the doorway of

141

the Majestic, protected by the half-open oak door. Ten yards along the street from the hotel stood Marcle's wagon, its shafts, free of horses, resting on the hardpack of the street. A metal plate had been lashed across the driver's seat protecting the men beneath the canvas cover.

One of the Volunteers must have spotted a cloud of dust. 'Old Sam's headin' this aways, Mr Tobin,' he called out.

Tobin turned to see the old soldier riding hard for the town, his body low over his mount's neck. Tobin could see him lashing at his horse urging the animal into an even greater speed. Tobin stepped out on to the boardwalk. A minute or so later the old soldier hauled back on the reins as his mount drew level with the sheriff's office. The horse skittered across the hardpack as Sam turned its head.

'They're comin', Mr Tobin!'

'How many they got, Sam?'

Sam was gasping, sucking in air. 'Twenty, I guess. Mebbe a few more.'

Tobin swore inwardly. He could only hope the Wilson brothers could pull off what they'd planned. 'You've done your share, Sam. Make sure you find somewhere safe.'

'Aw hell! Bear Creek's my town. I got my ol' scattergun, I'll stand with the cowboys across the street with Mr Bolton.'

'OK, glad to have you with us.'

Tobin turned away to snatch up his spyglass which he'd rested on the wooden chair outside his office. With his naked eye he could now see the dust cloud gathering a couple of miles from the town. He raised his spyglass, giving the barrel a quick turn to bring the approaching riders into focus. They were strung out in two lines one behind the other. He moved the spyglass a fraction but was unable to recognize Hayter or Masefield at this distance.

He'd never fooled himself that Hayter was the same as the

gun-crazy fools that he and Josh had dealt with in the past. Hayter was both intelligent and ruthless and he had Masefield with him to make sure the men followed orders. Watching the approaching riders break from the open country to the track leading to the town Tobin had a memory flash of a cavalry charge at Bull Run when Johnny Reb overran the Union forces, and only a handful of northern soldiers, himself included, escaped capture.

This time he knew his little force of ranch hands and Volunteers had the advantage of surprise, but if any of them were going to survive and protect the gold his plan had to work first time – there would be no second chances. He slid his Colt from its holster, spinning the chamber to check again that it was fully loaded. A sign of nerves, Josh would have said, and Tobin thought, not for the first time that day, he'd have given plenty to have Devlin standing with him now.

By now Hayter's men could easily be seen with the naked eye. Tobin picked up the red cloth and stepped from the boardwalk to duck behind a water trough. His eyes swept across the riders. Where the hell were Hayter and Masefield? He was damned sure they wouldn't be hanging back while their no-goods reached the gold. Tobin glanced behind him: the barrels of two Winchester long guns had appeared above the metal plate at the front of the wagon. The sharpshooters were readying themselves.

He turned to look back at the oncoming riders. Again he asked himself the question: where the hell were Hayter and Masefield? Kill them both and he'd wager that the rest would fall away. The riders were now maybe half a mile away. If he'd judged correctly he guessed that shooting would start as the riders hit Main Street. The two lines of men would be intent on scaring the townsfolk and driving a path to the jailhouse where they thought the gold was being kept. A rifle shot snapped out from one of the buildings.

'Hold your goddamned fire,' Wallace shouted. 'They're still outta range.'

But within a minute the riders had advanced close to the edge of town. Tobin saw both lines come to a halt maybe five hundred yards from the start of Main Street. The leading line of riders broke apart and a rider from the rear moved forward to take his position. Masefield! Amongst the other riders in their dirty range clothes Masefield stuck out like one of those fancy dummies in the shops back east. Tobin's mind raced. Hayter must be at the rear, both he and Masefield each taking charge of maybe a dozen men.

'They're comin' in!' Tobin yelled. 'Wait for the order to fire!'

Tobin saw Masefield dig his spurs cruelly into the sides of his mount, urging the animal forward. The line of riders alongside him took their cue from him and moved to flank him. Then Tobin saw that his plan with the Wilson brothers was going to fail. The second line of riders hadn't moved. Even as Masefield and his line of riders closed Main Street, the second line stood still, some five hundred yards from where the trail broke on to the start of the street.

Tobin's brain raced. 'Stand by to fire!'

His plan wasn't going to work but he knew he still had to get the timing right. Too soon and Masefield and his men would veer away to safety. Too late and they'd be on to the street. Tobin sucked air into his lungs and readied himself, his Colt gripped hard in his hand. Masefield and his men were maybe twenty yards away from Main Street, each man carrying either a long gun or a sidearm. Standing up, clear of the protection provided by the water trough, Tobin waved the red cloth to signal the Wilson brothers.

Along the street the voices of the Wilsons rang clear as they urged on their horses hidden from Tobin's view. From the dusty soil ten yards ahead of Masefield and his riders, a rope sprung chest high to the advancing line of riders. Shouted oaths rang out as a moment later the horses breasted the rope a few inches below their foaming mouths. The rope, stretched across the street, snapped taut. For a terrible moment Tobin thought that the momentum of the line of horses would drag the Wilson brothers across the street. Then the horse alongside Masefield stumbled, throwing the rider forward over the head of his mount.

The line collapsed as other horses were thrown to the ground, riders being catapulted into a maelstrom of flying hoofs. The air was torn with the noise of wounded horses, their tortured screams bouncing between the wooden buildings of the street. Above the din of men and horses Tobin's voice rang out across the street.

'Fire!'

For almost thirty seconds the townsmen of Bear Creek sent bullets raining down on the street below them. Marcle's sharpshooters cut down men rapidly and methodically. A few of the riders rolled from their mounts to run across the street, firing wildly, only to be cut down by the scatterguns of Bolton and his cowboys. Riderless horses ran around, eyes rolling in panic, as the barrage of shooting continued.

'Hold your fire!' Tobin yelled.

The din subsided, only broken by the heavy wheezing of injured horses and the groans of dying men face down in the dirt. Tobin stood up slowly. With a glance to the stationary line of riders beyond the town he walked slowly to the middle of the street. A few yards ahead of the fallen horses and the bodies of men a solitary figure lay face down in the dirt, blood staining the side of his head. The shiny boots, the leather vest, and the fine Stetson a few yards from the body told Tobin what he'd hoped to avoid: Masefield had cheated the hangman.

145

Tobin swung around, suddenly aware of his stupidity in standing in the middle of the street unprotected. But still the line of riders outside the town hadn't moved. Had they decided the gold was not worth dying for? Tobin could see Hayter now. As Masefield had been, he was in the centre of the line of a dozen men. He must know now that the odds were on the side of Bear Creek. He'd got the money from the ranches. Surely that would satisfy him.

Jesus Christ! The line of riders suddenly moved forward, the men firing as they advanced. Bullets smacked into the dirt of Main Street. Tobin felt the pressure of air as a slug missed him by inches. He broke into a run, clearing the trough with a leap, crashing hard into the dust. Bullets smacked against the trough, causing fountains of water to spray into the street. Tobin rolled over on his side, waving frantically in the direction of the wagon.

The canvas of the wagon was ripped aside. Above the iron plate, outlined in the early afternoon sun, was the unmistakable outline of multiple rotating gun barrels. Protected by the plate, the gunner crouched in the position he needed to fire. From the line of advancing riders, above the sound of gunshots, a shout went up.

'Gatling!'

Tobin swung around to see the line of Hayter's men, now only a few yards from Main Street frantically heaving on their horses' heads. The line broke, as the riders endeavoured only to escape the threat of two hundred rounds a minute coming towards them from the Gatling. Tobin thought he heard Hayter shouting orders, attempting to halt the panic, but the horses scattered in all directions. Some riders were hidden behind the end of the buildings at the edge of town before quickly reappearing as shots from the men in the side alley-ways rang out. Moments later all that could be seen was a

146

large dustcloud moving away from the town. Tobin managed a grim smile. Hayter, it appeared, had thrown in his hand – all his plans to steal the gold had come to nothing. Tobin scrambled to his feet as a loud cheer went up from the Volunteers and men began to appear on the roofs. He opened his mouth to shout but their captain was ahead of him.

'Get back to your places!' Wallace roared. 'I'll tell you when to move!'

Quickly, the men ducked down out of sight. Tobin turned to check that the riders were continuing to head north. The cloud of dust travelling further and further from the town told him they were no longer a threat to Bear Creek. A wave of relief swept through him as he felt his muscles relax.

'OK,' Tobin called. 'Stand down when Cap'n Wallace gives you the order.'

Tobin looked across towards the Majestic but there was no sign of Forbes, and he guessed that he was with McKenzie. He looked across to the wagon to see Marcle, his arm around Daley's shoulder, assisting the Company man to step down to the street. Tobin walked across to the wagon.

'You got hit?'

Daley swore. 'Goddamned ricochet! One of those damned no-goods got lucky. Took a slug straight through my leg.'

Tobin was about to reply when he heard the scream. For a second he was sure his heart missed a beat. He knew immediately: Elizabeth! Ignoring Daley, he whirled around and raced to the Majestic, his Colt grasped in his fist, thankful once again he'd always stuck to his army training and reloaded his sidearm. He charged up the steps from the street on to the boards and flung himself through the open door of the Majestic, his arm ramrod straight before him, his Colt ready to fire.

'Hold it there, Tobin!' Hayter shouted. 'Or this one dies now!'

Hayter, his arm around Forbes's neck, was shielded from Tobin's line of fire. Against the side of Forbes's head was pressed the barrel of Hayter's gun. A wild fury consumed Tobin. Forbes would have to take his chances. Right now Tobin's only concern was Elizabeth.

'Where is she?'

Hayter gave a short harsh laugh. He nodded in the direction of the corner of the vestibule and for an instant Tobin allowed his eyes to shift. In the corner the edge of a blue skirt and a woman's feet protruded from behind a chesterfield.

'If she's dead I swear I'll take three days to kill you,' Tobin's voice rasped as if a file had been drawn across a horse's hoofs. For a moment his Colt trembled in his hand.

'You'll not be killing anyone,' Hayter rasped. 'But maybe I'll kill this young fool.' He screwed the barrel of his gun harder into the side of Forbes's head. 'Tobin, you're gonna do as I say. You're gonna walk across to the jailhouse, fill a saddle-bag with gold, and bring it back here with a horse.'

'You're crazy, Hayter. You can kill us both. There's still a dozen men out there who'll shoot you down when you try to ride out.'

'Not if I take the lovely lady with me.'

'She's alive, Ben. In a swoon—' Forbes was cut off as Hayter tightened the grip on his throat.

'Shut your damned mouth, boy! Or you'll die now!'

From behind Tobin came the sound of someone treading on the boards outside the hotel. 'Stay where you are! I'll handle this!'

'I knew you'd see sense, Tobin,' Hayter sneered. 'I knew you could handle things.'

'Sure I can, you sonovabitch.'

Tobin's Colt roared. Blood spurted from Forbes's shoulder, the heavy slug spinning him around and sending him crashing to the floor. Hayter was thrown against the wall. For an instant he was in Tobin's line of fire. Tobin's Colt roared again. Blood spurted from Hayter's wrist, sending his sidearm arcing through the air above the motionless Forbes and falling to the carpet several feet away. Tobin stood ramrod straight, his arm extended, ready to fire again. The vestibule reeked of gunpowder, the air was heavy with blue smoke, and the silence only broken by Hayter's strangled cursing as he clutched at his smashed wrist. Slowly, Tobin lowered his gun.

Hayter looked across at Tobin, his face screwed up in agony. 'Goddamn you, Tobin. Co ahead, shoot me.'

For a moment or two Tobin didn't speak. Then he nodded. 'That's jest what I'm gonna do. I couldn't give a damn for some Company's gold. But you took the life of a good man.' He raised his arm once more. 'An' now you're gonna pay for it.'

'No, Ben!'

Elizabeth's voice cut through the air. Startled, Tobin glanced to the corner of the room. Elizabeth, ashen-faced, was standing behind the chesterfield. She was staring straight at him, shock registering in her eyes.

'Don't shoot him, Ben! I beg you.'

Tobin looked back at Hayter as if she hadn't spoken. 'You deserve to die!' His voice was loud, almost a shout. 'You preyed on fellow soldiers, sold them to the Confederates for food. You murdered my friend. You almost destroyed a good man here in this town. God knows what other evil you've caused.'

'Then he should answer in court, Ben.' There was a note of desperation in Elizabeth's voice. 'Please Ben, don't betray Josh Devlin.'

At the mention of Devlin's name, Tobin glanced again in the direction of Elizabeth. She managed a weak smile of encouragement. 'You'll be doing right, Ben. You know it.'

For several seconds there was silence in the room. Then

149

Tobin took a deep breath and slid his Colt into its holster. He stepped forward to place a hand roughly on Hayter's shoulder. 'I'm just damned sorry I'll not be around when you hang.'

CHAPTER FIFTEEN

Tobin stood on the boardwalk, Bolton alongside him. The range boss's shirt was bulked out with the strapping over a wound and his right arm was held across his body with a wide bandage. Both men were looking towards the edge of town where a group of riders heading west, all carrying long guns at the ready, surrounded the wagon rolling from the hard-pack of Main Street on to the trail to Cheyenne.

Tobin exhaled noisily. 'I gotta say, Mr Bolton, I'm damned pleased to see them Pinkertons rollin' outta Bear Creek.'

Bolton grinned. 'Guess the town's gonna be a lot quieter from now on.' He looked across the street to where half a dozen men were working on the fronts of the bank and the adjoining stores. 'Mr Wilkins tells me the Company's gonna be coverin' the ranch money an' fittin' a new safe in a coupla months.' He paused. 'Jest in case any other no-goods think they can pick up some easy money I'll write an' let you know when it's here. Then mebbe you'd think o' comin' back,' he added, his grin growing wider.

'I'm gonna be too busy,' Tobin said. 'Mayor Parker's got some thinkin' to do about law in this town. Anyways, all the no-goods are gonna stay away when they hear the name Bear Creek.' His hand went to his hat as Beth Garner and Janey came along the boardwalk towards them.

151

'Howdy Mrs Garner, Janey. Sure is a great day.'

'I heard you were soon to leave us, Mr Tobin. I've somethin' to say afore you leave.'

'Sure. Why don't we step into the office?'

Beth Garner looked at Bolton who raised a hand in salute to both women. He smiled at Janey. 'You care for some coffee, Miss Janey, 'cross at the Majestic while your ma talks to Mr Tobin?'

'Well, yes, Mr Bolton. I'd like that.'

'You gotta take my left arm,' Bolton said. 'That OK?'

Beth Garner and Tobin exchanged smiles as they watched for a moment the pair crossing the street heading towards the hotel. 'Reckon you might just be getting a newcomer to the family,' Tobin said. 'We'll walk along.'

'Take a seat, Mrs Garner,' Tobin said when they'd entered the office. He went around the desk and took his own seat. 'Now, what's this about?'

'I know Josh was your friend, and I think you ought to know.'

'If you're going to tell me that he was Janey's father, I'd already guessed.'

'Oh!' Beth Garner's surprised expression was replaced by a sad frown and a tightening of her lips. 'He asked me many times to marry him and I always refused. I wish I hadn't been so foolish.'

'You'll remember him in his prime. That's what he would have wanted.'

'I'd have been happy for us both to grow old together, Mr Tobin.'

'Josh wouldn't have grown old,' Tobin said softly. 'I asked Doc McKenzie this morning. I knew something about Josh. He had a slug sitting on his spine and it was moving. He'd have been dead within three months.'

Or maybe he could have lived for a few years, as McKenzie

152

had explained to Tobin that morning. But Devlin would have been helpless as a newborn child. After talking and thinking about what to do both men agreed this was something Beth Garner didn't need to know.

'Omigod! He never said—' Her voice trailed away, and she plucked a tiny white piece of lace from her sleeve and dabbed at her eyes.

'We'll both remember Josh as he was.' Tobin said firmly. 'He was brave, good humoured, an' don't forget he was a real fancy dresser.' He smiled. 'Josh would sure want us to remember that.'

Beth Garner managed a weak smile. 'Yes, he would.' She sighed. 'He had a fine and gentle way about him. Thank you Mr Tobin.'

After she'd left Tobin spent the next half hour writing up his account of the events of the previous days. Lawmen down in Cheyenne would want all the details. Anyways, Tobin realized, when he got back to Pittsburgh writing reports would be something with which he'd need to be familiar. Thinking of Pittsburgh brought Millie to mind, and the promise he'd made about taking her back east. He'd look damned foolish if what he was planning didn't work out. He wrote his signature at the bottom of the page and stowed away the journal in a drawer of the desk. Coffee would have to wait – he needed to talk to Bradden across at McKenzie's place.

McKenzie was poking around in the bottom of a saucer with a glass rod when Tobin stepped into the doctor's room. He looked up at Tobin and gave a wry smile.

'I'll miss you when you've gone back east. Treating townsfolk for fever and stuff will be too calm after these last weeks.' He poked again at the saucer. There was a metallic sound as the slug moved around. 'Got this one of yourn out with a single cut. I carry on like this and they'll be askin' for me at that hospital down at Cheyenne.'

Tobin leaned forward to look at the large slug. What was it that McKenzie had told him? Something about an Englishman by the name of Lister finding out how to stop gunshot wounds turning bad. In War some of the men alongside him would still be alive now if the doctors had known what McKenzie knew now.

The doctor nodded in the direction of the door. 'You can go through. Don't get 'em all worked up.'

Tobin pushed through the door and for a moment stood at the threshold, looking at the bunks on the opposite sides of the room. Bradden, pale and drawn was propped up against the bedhead, his eyes closed, apparently asleep. Opposite, Forbes lay on his back, looking at the stucco ceiling. He turned his head to look towards Tobin.

'Newspaperman from Cheyenne came in afore noon,' Forbes said, his voice sounding strained. 'Gonna make me a hero, he said. I tol' him a story like one of those Ned Buntline yarns I useda read.'

Tobin laughed. 'He came an' saw me. I tol' him he was gonna go swimmin' in the horse trough he didn't vamoose.' His laugh trailed away. 'How's the shoulder?'

'Hurts like hell.'

'I hope you ain't gonna hold it agin me.'

'No chance o' that, Ben. That sonovabitch Hayter woulda killed us both. He had a straight line to our office from the Majestic. He was plannin' to take us both down with him. I was lucky to be there when he came in at the back of the hotel.'

Tobin made a mouth. 'Don't get lucky like that too often.'

'I'm lucky to have Doc McKenzie. He reckons I'll be up an' about in a few days.'

'An' I've got good news. Mayor Parker says the councilmen have voted to keep you on as sheriff. Seems they can do that without the town havin' a vote.'

'Townsfolk might not like that.'

'Not what I've been hearin'. They reckon you been treadin' in Josh Devlin's tracks real fine.'

'Well, I'm damned! Almost worth gettin' shot for.'

Tobin was about to speak when a noise came from the opposite side of the room. He looked over to see Bradden, his eyes open, attempting to speak.

'What is it, Mr Bradden?' Tobin crossed the room to stand by Bradden's bed.

'I wanna try an' explain.'

As before, Tobin picked up the cane chair at the bedside and spun it around so he could sit with his arms resting on the chair back.

'You tol' me the other day you'd been Hayter's spy.'

'Bradden! What the hell you been doin'?' Forbes's voice, although weak, reached the two men.

'Hayter made me do it,' Bradden said in a low voice. 'I swear I had no choice.'

'What did he have on you?' Tobin asked.

Bradden pressed his lips into a thin line and turned his head away from Tobin as if determined not to answer the question. Then at Tobin's next question he looked back at Tobin, startled.

'Was he with you during the War?'

'How did you know that?'

'What was he? Your officer, mebbe your sergeant?'

'Sergeant,' Bradden said. His voice was near to cracking.

'An' I'm guessin' you were both taken by Johnny Reb at Ball's Bluff an' sent to Andersonville.'

Bradden's head twitched as if he was shooing off a fly. 'Where you getting' all this from?'

Tobin ignored the question. He leaned forward and glared at Bradden across the chairback. 'An' in prison I reckon you were a goddamned Raider, preyin' on men who had fought alongside you. Mebbe men who'd saved your skin.'

Save for a brief gasp of shock from Forbes there was silence in the room for several seconds before Bradden spoke.

'I swear to you I was no Raider. You don't know what it was like in that hellhole. It was dog eat dog! I was young and scared. Hayter said he'd protect me. Keep me alive if I got sick or get me food when I was hungry. I swear I just looked after what he an' the others got their hands on.'

'That wasn't all, Bradden,' Tobin pressed on. 'You betrayed George Devlin to Johnny Reb.'

'No! No! I swear that wasn't me.'

'Then who was it?'

Bradden hesitated. 'I give you a name, he'll have me killed. You'll never hold him behind bars.'

Tobin looked at him for a few seconds. 'You don't give me a name, I'm gonna fix it so you're headin' for a hangin'. I'm gonna ask you one more time. Who sold out Josh Devlin's brother?'

Bradden's tongue flickered over his lips, his eyes screwed shut. Then he opened them and spoke, a note of resignation in his voice. 'Max Hayter. He got two bottles of French wine for himself an' Frank Masefield.'

'You ready to swear that in front of a judge?'

Bradden nodded.

'Let me hear you say the words.'

'Yes, I'll swear it in front of a judge.' Bradden looked from beneath his brow at Tobin. 'The Gatling was broke when I got it from the gunshop.'

'I know. I took a look afore it came to you.' Tobin smiled

156

grimly. 'It still ain't fixed but Hayter an' his no-goods didn't know that.'

Tobin leaned back. He'd got what he wanted. Hayter had been responsible for the deaths of both Devlin brothers. With a witness to the betrayal in Andersonville, and Forbes's evidence about the death of Josh Devlin there was no chance of Hayter beating the hangman when he came up for trial.

'You gonna put me in jail?' Bradden's face was chalk-white.

'No, I ain't. You weren't a Raider. You were a scared boy.'

'You think the army's gonna believe that just cos we're a dozen years on? They'll take me back east. You don't know the law back there.'

'But I do, Mr Bradden. You'll not be goin' east.' He stood up. 'I'm told you're a fine councilman, Mr Bradden, an' Miss Peabody's gonna remember your courage for the rest of her life.'

'There's a lot more to bein' sheriff than I ever guessed,' Forbes said slowly, as he managed to raise a hand as Tobin left the room.

Tobin was approaching Elizabeth's house when he saw the two cowboys standing a few yards from her gate. One of the men held the bridle of a handsome Appaloosa, the coat of the animal showing white with a sprinkling of irregular black spots. As Tobin got a clearer look at the men's faces below their battered hats he recognized the two cowboys he'd scared off the day he'd first been heading for Bear Creek.

'We wuz hopin' to see Miss Elizabeth,' the taller one said, as Tobin reached the gate. 'We wanna say how sorry we are, actin' stupid like we did.'

'I'll ask if Miss Elizabeth will see you,' Tobin said brusquely.

The two cowboys reached up to pull off their hats as, a few

minutes later, Tobin came down to the gate with Elizabeth on his arm.

'Say what you gotta say,' said Tobin.

The taller of the two stepped a yard closer to the gate. 'Me an' Fred here, we wanna say how sorry we are about what we did on the trail them weeks back. We ain't like that an' I don't know what we wuz thinkin'. Anyways, we hope you'll accept this pony as a gift, an' forgive us for bein' foolish.' The speaker lowered his head, and both men shuffled around in the loose dirt, their eyes cast down.

Elizabeth looked at Tobin, her eyebrows raised, before she turned back to face the men. 'I accept your apologies. The pony is beautiful.' She looked straight at the man. 'How is your arm?'

Recognizing that he and his companion had been forgiven the speaker lost his worried expression. 'Cost me a lump o' flesh, ma'am, but it'll be OK.'

'Then if you'll take the pony to the livery stable for me we'll never mention this again.'

'Sure, ma'am,' the cowboy said, nodding his head furiously. 'That's mighty generous.'

The two men, now apparently anxious to be away, turned the head of the pony and strode briskly in the direction of Main Street.

'They ain't bad, just stupid sometimes,' Tobin said, as they turned back to the house. 'I've heard that Millie makes coffee about this time,' he said. 'How is she now?'

'The bruises still show but they'll be gone in a few days. Doctor McKenzie has been splendid.'

Five minutes later they were both seated in the parlour, a tray on a low table between them holding cups and saucers and a coffee pot. Millie paused at the door and gave a little bob in the direction of Elizabeth.

'Should I close the door, ma'am?'

'You're not to smile when you ask that, Millie.' Elizabeth's own smile taking the sting out of her words. 'I've mentioned this before. Do please remember no unmarried lady sits in a room with a gentleman behind a closed door. The young ladies in Cheyenne will be quite put out.'

The smile disappeared from Millie's face. 'Yes, ma'am. Sorry, ma'am.'

Tobin, amused by the girl, waited until he was alone with Elizabeth before taking the chair opposite. 'First time I heard of a clapboard having a drawing room was from Millie,' he said. 'You're trainin' her well.'

'I'll be sorry to lose her. I'll be sorry to lose you, too. When do you plan to leave?'

'I'm takin' the stage to Cheyenne in a few days,' Tobin said, 'then I'll pick up the railroad.'

'Pittsburgh will be very different from Bear Creek.'

'A mite quieter, I hope.'

'What will you do there?'

Instead of replying directly he thrust his hand into the pocket of his leather vest and pulled out a metal badge. He handed it across to Elizabeth who held it so the light from the window was thrown on to its shiny surface. She examined it carefully for a few seconds.

'Is the crest from your family?'

'That's the crest of the English Earl of Chatham. His family name was Pitt, and he gave his name to Pittsburgh.'

'So is it a keepsake of some kind?'

'No, ma'am. Every police agent in the city has worn that badge since '73.'

'You mean. . . ?'

'The city's gonna have a new detective force. Just like they have in London, England.'

'And are you going to work for this new detective force?'

'You could say that. I'm gonna head it.'

Elizabeth's eyes widened. 'My, oh, my!' A shadow flickered across her even features. 'Then you'll not be returning to Bear Creek for a while.'

'No. I'm gonna be busy for a few years, mebbe a lot more.' Tobin paused, reached across the table, and took her hand. 'That's why I'm askin' you to come with me.'

Startled, Elizabeth withdrew her hand and turned away looking towards the window. 'What happened—' she stopped for a second before trying again. 'What happened between us at Ellisville. . . .'

'What happened between us made me sure I wanted you to be my wife.'

For a few seconds Elizabeth appeared unable to speak. Then, 'Do you know how old I am?'

Tobin smiled. 'A coupla years younger than me, I guess.' He leaned forward to take both her hands in his. 'I'd like your answer, Elizabeth. I can't stay in Bear Creek. I've work to do back east an' I must leave real soon. Will you be my wife and live in Pittsburgh?'

Elizabeth's face was pink with pleasure. 'Yes, Ben, oh yes!'

'An' I've another notion. If her pa agrees we'll take your little friend Emma Ruskin as you promised.'

Elizabeth's face lit up. 'I'll start my music class again. Emma will be my finest pupil!'

'We'll have someone to work around the house. An' there's somethin' else. You'll need your own maid. Millie would be fine.'

As they both leaned forward to each other there was a shriek of joy from out in the hallway. Then the door behind them was firmly closed.

160